FARMINGTON COMMUNITY LIBRARY

IN MEMORY OF:
JUDY PEIFFER

GIVEN BY:
CARRIE PEIFFER

SEP 22 2006

His Brother's Guns

**Center Point
Large Print**

**This Large Print Book carries the
Seal of Approval of N.A.V.H.**

His Brother's Guns

Wayne C. Lee

Center Point Publishing
Thorndike, Maine

This Center Point Large Print edition
is published in the year 2005 by arrangement with
Golden West Literary Agency.

Copyright © 1958 by Arcadia House.
Copyright © renewed 1986 by Wayne C. Lee.

The text of this Large Print edition is unabridged. In other
aspects, this book may vary from the original edition. Printed in
Thailand. Set in 16-point Times New Roman type.

ISBN 1-58547-665-X

Library of Congress Cataloging-in-Publication Data

Lee, Wayne C.
    His brother's guns / Wayne C. Lee.--Center Point large print ed.
        p. cm.
    ISBN 1-58547-665-X (lib. bdg. : alk. paper)
    1. Large type books. I. Title.

PS3523.E34457H57 2005
813'.54--dc22

                                                          2005012865

CHAPTER I

Sometimes a man can't see trouble before it hits him. Too often it steals up on him so silently he can't even hear it. But there are times when a man can feel it and, though he can't say what it is or where it will strike or when, knows it is coming as surely as night follows day.

Matt Freeman had that feeling as he ducked his head against the chilling March wind and urged his horse along the road paralleling crooked Tumbleweed Creek. It was more then just the cutting wind that made him shiver beneath his heavy coat. That north wind sweeping down over the southwestern Nebraska prairies could cut to the marrow of a man's bones. But as the sun reached its zenith, the day warmed. Yet Matt didn't. And he knew that the chill inside him wasn't all the fault of the wind.

Through the afternoon, as he came nearer to Tumbleweed, the uneasiness grew in him. Tumbleweed was a little town, his brother Fred had said in his letters, and it was just as unsettled as its name implied. But Fred hadn't mentioned any serious trouble afoot. That uneasiness inside Matt now suggested something vital and urgent.

The sun gave up its effort to bring spring to the brown prairie and settled toward the horizon, hitting Matt full in the face before disappearing and giving the winter-dry grass a reddish hue. With the sunset, the wind went down, fading to a mere whisper. The night chill crept in on Matt, making him pull his coat tighter around him.

He glanced up at the sandhills to the south and thought of riding up there. The air there would be just as cold but it would be dry. Here next to the creek the air was damp, and the cold penetrated like a sharp knife.

To the north, across the creek, the prairie was flat and stretched away as far as the eye could see. Two worlds, Matt thought. Flat prairie that would make good farmland to the north; land the ranchers would try to hold for its rich buffalo grass. To the south, sandhills, sagebrush, bunch grass and little valleys of the richest grass of all; the sodbuster would tear it up and these winds would blow the loose sand away. Two worlds, and it would take two kinds of people to run them. But each kind would try to rule it all.

Maybe that was the trouble Matt felt in his bones. Fred had hinted that there was some strife between the ranchers who had been here for years and the new surge of homesteaders coming in. Matt shook his head. That wasn't it. He had seen the struggle between farmer and rancher before. This was different. Maybe it had to do with Fred's flour mill. Or maybe it was the key in his pocket, a key that would open a box he had never seen. A man had been killed getting that key to him. He could only guess what the box contained. And guessing was such a futile pastime that he had spent little time thinking about it.

6

He spent no time on it now. Ahead, he could see lights beginning to appear, cutting tiny holes through the deepening dusk. That would be Tumbleweed. Matt urged his horse to a long trot. A good warm meal and bed would rid him of this depressing mood.

There was no light in the first house he approached, a low, nearly flat-roofed soddy. Nor was there any light in the next houses. Matt reined down to a walk. There were lights ahead, all right, but they were pretty well bunched and they weren't the steady lights of kerosene lamps. They flickered and tossed like pieces of bark on rough water.

After he had passed another dark house, Matt pulled to a halt. Maybe here was the trouble he had been feeling. He could see now that those lights were torches. He hadn't come to Tumbleweed looking for trouble, and now he hung back, hesitant to ride ahead and maybe get sucked into something that was none of his affair.

He sat quietly for a long minute, a tall man, a hundred and eighty pounds of bone and hard muscle. Working in a flour mill had done nothing to soften his muscles. His gray eyes turned toward the torches, seemed to penetrate the darkness. His hand slid down over his thigh, a habit not yet broken. But there was no gun there. There hadn't been for several months now.

He was concentrating so much on the milling men with the torches that he failed to notice the movement beside the house close by. Only when he heard the voice did he jerk his attention back. And again his hand wiped across his hip where there was no gun.

"You're not intending to ride down there, are you, stranger?"

Matt's eyes bored through the gloom at the girl standing by the corner of the house. Finding a girl challenging him startled him more than the question she asked.

"Been debating that myself," he said slowly.

"I wouldn't do it," she said, "unless you're looking for trouble."

He liked her voice. It was soft now, as though she didn't want any other chance listener to hear her. And there was worry in it, too. Matt wished he could get a good look at her face. Maybe it would be as pretty as her voice. All he could tell was that she was small; he'd guess nearly a foot shorter than he was. Yet her voice didn't suggest a youngster.

"I don't like trouble," he said after a minute. "But I do like to know what's going on."

The girl sighed. "Curiosity killed the cat, you know."

"I've heard of it killing bigger things than cats. Is that what you mean?"

"You can draw your own conclusions. Right now you're in no trouble and no one is crowding you. The road leads right back the way you came."

He chuckled. "So it does. You're making a right powerful argument for me to vamoose. The trouble is, I'm cold and hungry. And I've got some of that curiosity that augered the cat."

8

"Whose side will you be on when you get down there?"

Matt looked back at the torches. They were still bobbing around, and he thought he could hear a man's voice shouting. "What sides do I have to choose from?" he asked.

"If you don't know that, what are you doing in town tonight?"

"I just came up the river from McCook. I didn't come looking for a war."

The girl stepped closer and peered into Matt's face. Matt returned the scrutiny, liking what he saw. Maybe it was the shadows, but he was sure her eyes were as black as the night around them. Her small nose, turned up a little at the end, and lips which were parted slightly as she studied him rounded out as pretty a face as he had ever seen.

"Maybe you *are* just a drifter," she said, stepping back.

He jerked himself back to reality. Probably she wouldn't be that pretty when the light of day struck her.

"I'm not exactly drifting, ma'am," he said. "But I've never been here before."

"You don't carry a gun, I see," she said, eyes sliding down over him.

"Like I said, I'm not looking for trouble. Guns always seem to drag you into trouble sooner or later."

She nodded vigorously. "That's right. And that's what is liable to happen down there tonight."

"Is that a gun party?" Matt asked, jerking a thumb toward the flickering torches.

"There are plenty of guns there. And quick tempers to go with them."

"Looks like they might be fixing to burn something."

The girl nodded. "They are. They're set on burning the mill."

Matt stiffened. The only thing in the entire town that held any interest for him was the flour mill. When his brother, Fred, had mentioned in his letters that there was some trouble brewing, Matt had figured it was probably a personal issue between Fred and some other hothead. For Fred, though usually right, was too quick-tempered for his own good.

"Any reason for burning the mill?" Matt asked, in a hurry now to get what information he could before riding down into that mob. For he was going. He knew that.

"They think they have good reasons," the girl said. "They say there'll be no peace along the Tumbleweed as long as that mill operates."

Matt nodded. Maybe Fred's hint of trouble wasn't a personal thing, after all. This sounded like the old feud between ranchers and settlers, only this time, Matt could easily become one of the principal figures. For he had no intention of running out on Fred. And from the looks of things down by the creek, Fred needed help right now.

"Excuse me, ma'am," he said as carelessly as possible. "Think I'll ride down and see what the hassle is all about."

He nudged his horse into a long trot before the girl could object. The street turned straight toward the creek between two rows of business houses. Between buildings, Matt caught glimpses of the torches down at the mill. Then, after passing a church, the road turned directly toward the mill, dropping sharply down the slope to the creek bank.

He put his horse to a faster gait. The angry murmur of men's voices was clear now. But still the torches had not touched the mill. He wondered what could be holding the men back, unless it was Fred. In that case, his place was there beside his brother.

He dismounted at the edge of the crowd, surprised that there were so few. He had expected at least twenty or thirty. Usually a mob bent on destruction, whether it be property or life, thrived on numbers. There were no more than a dozen carrying torches here. And two men stood on the loading platform in front of the big sliding door of the mill. Those men were arguing violently with the torch bearers.

Matt hesitated. One of those men up there ought to be Fred. But he had never seen either man before. Both men were tall, over six feet, and one was heavy-set. The torches caught the light of battle in the heavy man's pale blue eyes and reflected from the marshal's badge pinned to his shirt front.

The other man was as tall as the marshal but he was thin. He appeared calm, and he carried himself as straight as a preacher in a pulpit. His hat was off and his brown hair was still unruffled. Both men held guns in their hands.

"You'd better go home, Bull," the thinner man on the platform said in a smooth, persuasive voice. "You won't gain a thing by burning the mill."

"That ain't the way I figure it, Jok," a big man at the front of torch bearers rumbled. "We've had enough of this mill. It's the only thing that's keeping the sod-busters here."

Matt took a quick look at the man called Bull. He was dark-skinned, with black hair and eyes, and he was as heavy as the marshal although he was at least a couple of inches shorter.

"Better break it up before I blast a couple of you," the marshal growled, fingering his gun threateningly.

Matt's attention came back to the men with the torches. One of those torches was being used as a finger now to point at Jok. The man handling it was almost an exact replica of the man called Bull except that he was a little shorter and a little lighter and, Matt guessed, at least thirty years younger.

"This is none of your affair, Jok. We ranchers have got our fill of sodbusters and we're going to run them out. We're starting by burning this mill. You'd better get out of the way if you want to live to swindle any-body else out of his money."

The man on the platform frowned. "Careful what you say, Gyp. We intend to settle this peaceably."

"If he wants it otherwise," the marshal said significantly, "that's all right with me."

Matt watched the men crowding in. They paid no attention to the marshal. Matt guessed quickly that they feared nothing from the marshal so long as Jok didn't turn him loose. Jok was the power here. But Jok, even with the marshal's help, wasn't going to be enough. Matt could see it in the set faces of the men. They meant to burn the mill, and the two men on the platform weren't going to stop them. Another look at those two men, and Matt guessed that if they couldn't stop the mob short of force, they would back down. Jok obviously wasn't a man to engage in open violence.

Matt pushed forward. Fred must be out of town somewhere, and he had left the mill in the hands of this man who had employed the marshal to help. But few men were willing to fight to the death for someone else's property. These men wouldn't. It was up to Matt to take Fred's place and try to swing the balance of force the other way.

A hush dropped over the crowd as Matt swung up on the platform beside Jok. The absence of a gun on his hip was conspicuous now. He longed for the feel of his heavy .45, but all he had to fight with were words and fists.

"Need a little help persuading them?" Matt said to Jok.

Jok nodded slowly. "Seems as though I'm not having too much luck. But maybe you ought to think twice before taking a hand in this."

"I don't figure we've got much time to think about it."

"Who are you?" Bull demanded from the front ranks of the mob. "What are you horning in for?"

"I'll fix him," Gyp yelled, and threw his torch at Matt.

Matt sidestepped quickly, feeling the hot breath of the torch as it brushed past him and slammed against the door of the mill. He wheeled, picking up the torch. If the mill had been running today there would be wheat dust behind that door, and the dust might explode like gunpowder if a flame like this torch got to it.

Torch in hand, he wheeled back toward the mob and threw the torch straight at Gyp. Gyp screamed and dropped flat, letting the torch go over his head. When he got up, he was clawing at his gun, but Jok stopped him.

"Hold it, Gyp!" Jok said sharply. "You asked for that. Give him a chance to say why he's butting in."

"I know who he looks like," one man back in the crowd shouted. "Fred Freeman."

"I've got a right to look like him," Matt said. "I'm his brother."

A sudden hush fell. Finally Gyp broke the stillness.

"Another Freeman," he shouted. "Let's get rid of him."

"Shut up!" Bull snapped, and the younger man turned and scowled at Bull but said nothing more.

Jok took advantage of another silence to step up to

the edge of the platform and get the attention of the men.

"I think it's time we broke up this party, don't you? Go home and sleep on it. Come in tomorrow if you still feel the same way about it and we'll have a reasonable talk."

"Reasonable, he says!" Gyp blurted, and Bull swung a hand back across Gyp's face.

The younger man swore but said nothing more as Bull glowered at him.

"Reckon we'll do that," Bull said. "And we may feel just the same, too."

"That's your privilege," Jok said, and stood watching while the men turned away, some grumbling and some going in silence.

"Seems like I sort of unwound their tails by telling them who I was," Matt said as the last of the men put out his torch and faded into the night.

"You certainly did," Jok said, lighting up a cigarette with a hand that shook just a trifle.

"They wasn't looking for another Freeman," the marshal said.

Jok took a deep drag on his cigarette, then held out a hand to Matt. "I presume you're Matt Freeman. I've heard Fred speak of you often. I'm Preston Jok. I have a law office here in town, and I'm also locator for homesteaders looking for good land."

Matt shook the lawyer's hand. "You did Fred a good turn tonight—you and the marshal here."

"This is Marshal Pete Guckert," Jok introduced him.

"It's his job to keep law and order in Tumbleweed."

"Where is Fred?" Matt asked after shaking hands with the marshal.

The lawyer hesitated.

"I hate to tell you this, Matt," Jok said, "but Fred was killed today in a gun fight."

For a moment Matt felt as if he'd been kicked in the stomach by a mule. He leaned back against the side of the mill and didn't say anything for a while. Jok went on:

"That's why Pete and I were down here tonight stalling off that mob. Fred said you were to get the mill if anything ever happened to him. I didn't intend to turn over a pile of ashes."

"What happened?" Matt asked finally.

"Fred has been having trouble with Gyp Sanford for quite a while. It came to a head today. I didn't see it, but those who did said it was a fair fight. Gyp is mighty fast with a gun."

"That the jasper that threw the torch at me?"

Jok nodded. "He's the one. I reckon he figured you'd be after his hide as soon as you found out and he wanted to beat you to the punch. He might have done it, too, if it hadn't been for his Dad, Bull. And then you didn't have a gun."

"Would that make any difference to him?"

Jok shook his head. "You're a shrewd judge of men, aren't you? I doubt if it would make much difference to Gyp. It would make a lot of difference to Bull. But you were safe tonight. Gyp isn't one to get in bad with

16

the whole country if there's a way he can get his dirty work done without others knowing for sure he's responsible."

Matt nodded. "I reckon that pegs Gyp Sanford pretty well. What was the quarrel between Fred and him about?"

"A girl, Suzy Jensen. Daughter of one of the settlers out here. Gyp is sweet on her, in spite of the fact he's set on running the settlers out of the valley."

"Was it because of the settlers they were trying to burn the mill?"

Jok nodded. "The farmers have been getting their wheat ground into flour here and living on that when they couldn't get a decent price for their grain. The ranchers figure if they get rid of the mill, most of the settlers will have to pull out."

Matt sighed. "I doubt it," he said. "Where's Fred?"

"Up at Falley's hardware," Jok said, jumping off the platform. "Falley makes what caskets are needed around here. Funeral is tomorrow afternoon. Better come up and get a room in the hotel."

Matt shook his head. "As long as I own this mill now, I think I'll stay right here and see that nothing happens to it."

Jok nodded. "Good idea. Come on, Pete. See you tomorrow, Matt."

Matt watched the lawyer and the marshal disappear up the street.

CHAPTER II

Matt found the door to the little office which was built onto the front of the mill and tried it. It was unlocked. Inside, he struck a match, found a lantern and lit it. There was nothing here that wasn't absolutely essential. A small desk and chair with some pads of paper and a pencil. And over in front of the little window was a balance shaft and weights. Apparently the wagon scales were just outside.

Matt turned away and made a short tour of the mill, holding the lantern high as he glanced over the machinery and bins. Beside the office he found another room built against the mill. This had been Fred's living quarters, he discovered. It was small and cramped but it would do, Matt decided. There was a cot, a small stove, a cupboard, and a little table with a stool slid under it.

Matt went back outside and put his horse in a shed beside the mill that Fred had apparently used for a barn. After caring for his horse, Matt dragged himself wearily back into the living quarters. He considered cooking some supper, but that cot looked too inviting. He'd cook an extra big breakfast. Now he just wanted to pull off his boots and get to sleep.

It was cold in the little room, but Matt barely noticed it. He had slept out on nights that were as cold as this. And the walls so close around him gave him a false feeling of warmth and security.

But he didn't drop off to sleep as he had thought he would. The bad news Jok had given him was too fresh in his mind. And that mob trying to burn the mill was still clear in his memory. Before blowing out the lantern, he had taken Fred's rifle down from the hooks above the door and leaned it against the head of his bed.

When he finally managed to push thoughts of Fred from his mind, other things poured into the void.

For a couple of months he had been planning to come to Tumbleweed to try to sell Fred on the idea of installing rollers in place of stone burs in the mill.

But in spite of his determination to come out and work with Fred, he probably wouldn't have been here yet had it not been for the request of a dying man; a man Matt had never seen. The man had ridden into Jesse Prill's farm about four miles outside Stony Creek and had asked for Matt.

As Jesse told Matt later, the man was almost dead. He had been shot and had been riding for more than a day, holding a rolled up rag against the wound. When Jesse told him that Matt was in town, he had asked to send a message.

"He knew he couldn't last till I came to town after you," Jesse told Matt the next day. "He said he was a friend of Fred's. He wouldn't tell me who shot him, although I'm sure he knew. Just said it was somebody I didn't know and wouldn't care about. Seems like he'd got into some trouble and somehow got hold of an important box. He was afraid somebody would try to get it from him, so he took it to Fred."

"What was in the box?" Matt had asked.

"Don't know," Jesse said. "He didn't say. I ain't sure he knew himself. Guess he didn't trust Fred completely, either. Anyway, he gave me a key. Said it would open the box. He said Fred had always told him if he ever got in trouble and couldn't get to him, he should ride here to Stony Creek and get you."

"Seems like he thought he'd lay low for a while, then go back and get the box. But this fellow, whoever he was, found him and shot him. But the fellow didn't kill him and didn't get the key. He had it hid in his boot. He said he didn't dare go back to Tumbleweed, so he headed this way. Got as far as my place and knew he was going to pass on, so he stopped. Asked me to give this key to you."

"What am I supposed to do with it?" Matt asked.

"Take it back to Tumbleweed, get the box from Fred, and open it, I reckon. This fellow seemed to think it was mighty important to somebody that the right fellow get hold of what's in that box."

"How am I to know who the right person is?"

Jesse shrugged. "I don't have the slightest idea. Guess you're on your own. Maybe what's in the box will tell you who should get it."

Matt had thought of refusing to take the key. But what could he do? If he didn't take it, Jesse would be stuck with it. It wasn't Jesse's problem. It wasn't Matt's, either. Still, since the box had been left with Fred, he felt some responsibility. And Jesse couldn't go to Tumbleweed and take the key to Fred. He had a wife and three kids to take care of, and a farm to manage. Matt could go any time. Uncle Jed didn't need him now. Early spring wasn't a busy time at the mill.

"Must be something important for a man to risk his life to protect it," Matt had mused.

"I guess it is," Jesse said. "That fellow either didn't know just how important the things in that box were, or he was afraid to tell me."

"Didn't even give you a clue?"

Jesse shook his head. "None whatsoever. He blacked out just after he turned the key over to me and I'd promised I'd give it to you. He mumbled a little after that, but it didn't make sense. He never came to again."

Matt had taken the key, and the next day he had started for Tumbleweed.

Sleep came at last, but it wasn't the sound restful sleep that should have followed a hard day in the saddle such as he had had. His ear, even in sleep, was half tuned for sounds that would indicate the marauders were back. But nothing violated the stillness of the night.

After a big breakfast that tasted good even if Matt didn't appreciate his own cooking, he made a methodical though hurried examination of the mill. He found the machinery in good working order and wheat in the bin ready to be scoured and tempered for grinding. But he didn't find a trace of a box.

After giving the mill the once-over, Matt headed toward town. In the daylight he could see that the town lay mostly downstream from the mill and the dam, with most of it up on the banks to the south of the creek. The road he followed angled up the slope until it crossed the main street of the town which ran north and south. He turned up this street.

A church stood on his right, at the top of the slope, facing east. Across from it was a hardware store. On the east side of the street were several business places, including a drug store, barber shop, bank, Jok's law offices and a hotel. A grocery store was next to the church on the west side of the street. Then followed a new building that seemed to be empty, a general store, the marshal's office which had a tiny jail in the back, a saddle shop, and a blacksmith shop. Down at the far end of the street was a livery barn with a big corral behind it and a huge stack of prairie hay on the south side.

It looked like a nice peaceful town, Matt thought as he moved up the street.

He stopped in at the hardware for a minute to talk to Falley, the owner. He asked about Fred.

"Sure, we got him here," Falley said. "I don't do the undertaking. I just make the caskets. Handy to have them right here across from the church. Most of the funerals are at the church."

Matt wandered on down the street, stopping in stores, talking a little, listening more. It was a town divided in opinion. Serious trouble between plowmen and the saddlemen hadn't started yet, but the seeds had been planted and, if Matt were any judge, those seeds had sprouted well.

It was mid-morning when he came out of the blacksmith shop where he had loafed for an hour listening to the smithy talk to the owner of the livery stable, who was getting a horse shod. The livery owner had gone back to his barn which was across the street and south, the last building before the town gave way to the prairie. Now he was standing in front of his stable, and he motioned to Matt. Matt moved across to him.

"Thought you might as well look over my establishment, too," he said amiably. "I see you're giving the town the once-over."

"I guess that's right," Matt said. "Didn't suppose anybody would notice, though."

The livery owner laughed. "You'll have to be pretty sly to pull something I don't see. My name's Sid Bolling, in case you didn't get it over at the smithy."

Matt shook hands. "Guess you know who I am."

"Sure," Bolling said, leading the way into a room in the front of the barn that looked as if it were used for both office and harness repair room. "Saw you last night down at the mill."

Matt's forehead pulled into a frown. "Were you in that gang that tried to burn the mill?"

Bolling laughed. "I was there but I wasn't carrying no torch."

Matt looked at the short, paunchy man as he dropped in a chair and motioned to another chair for

Matt. His blue eyes were about the sharpest Matt had ever seen, seeming to look right through him.

"Maybe you could fill me in on what's been going on around here," Matt suggested. "It seems that I own the mill now, and I'd like to know how I'm going to get along here."

Bolling leaned back in his chair, the look of anticipation on his face reminding Matt of a cat eyeing a saucer of milk.

"I reckon I can tell you as much about what's been going on around here as anybody you'll find," he said. "What's pestering you?"

"Seems like somebody was pretty set on getting rid of the mill last night. What's behind that?"

"Same old scrap that goes on wherever settlers move into ranching territory. Only here the mill seems to be the one thing that is licking the ranchers."

"Why the mill? The farmers can sell their grain anywhere, can't they?"

"That's just it." Bolling paused to light his old blackened pipe. "About the only place within reasonable hauling distance where the farmers can sell their grain is Meadows, eighteen miles down the creek. Only when they get there, they can't get a decent price for their grain."

"How come?"

"Nobody knows." Bolling pointed the stem of his pipe at Matt. "But if you ask me, I'd say these ranchers have got the elevator man there, Dobson, bribed. If he won't give the farmers anything for their grain, they're going to starve out. That's how the ranchers figure it. But along comes this mill and grinds their wheat, and they live on that. Pretty hard to starve a man out as long as he's got some cows to milk, eggs, chickens and flour to use. So they figure they'll get rid of the mill, and the settlers will have to move on sooner or later."

"Surely other markets will develop," Matt suggested.

"Maybe," Bolling conceded. "But it's pretty hard for anything to grow in frigid weather. And you can bet that anybody who tries to set up a market for the farmers' stuff is going to get a mighty cold reception from the ranchers."

"Then the mill is in the front line of this fight," Matt said thoughtfully.

Bolling nodded. "All the heavy guns will be aimed right at it. Of course, you could close down the mill and everything would be peaceful."

"How would the settlers feel about that?"

"About like you would if somebody cut off your right arm."

"Was that part of the trouble behind the fight between Fred and Gyp Sanford yesterday?"

Bolling shook his head slowly. "Not on the face of things, anyway. Gyp has been sweet on Walt Jensen's girl, and she's flirted enough to lead him along. Then she got Fred to trailing her like a bucket calf. That's what they fought over. I ain't so sure that was the whole thing, though. Gyp wanted to get rid of Fred, and the mill as much as he did the competition for Suzy Jensen."

"What kind of a girl is this Suzy Jensen?"

"Pretty as sin and she knows it. She's got every single galoot and some that ain't single following her around like sick cats."

"Speaking of girls, I ran into one here last night as I rode into town. She was rather small and mighty pretty, too. It was dark but I think she had black eyes."

Bolling nodded. "You must have bumped into Jennie Kent. She was in town last night, but she wasn't down at the mill. At least I didn't see her there. She's a niece of Bull Sanford's. Lives with them on the Broken S and teaches school here. If you'll watch from your mill, you'll probably see her come and go from school."

Matt recalled the face he had seen in the dusk last night and he couldn't resist asking more about Jennie Kent. "She sides with Sanford in this trouble, I suppose?"

"Couldn't do otherwise and live in the same house with him. But she's different. Bull Sanford is about as civilized as an old one-horned bull. And his boy, Gyp, is worse. But Jennie is well educated. She fits in with Bull and Gyp about like a rose in a thistle patch. She's against all this fighting."

Matt let the old fellow ramble on, telling about the town and the country around it.

"Do you know of any man around here who has come up missing lately?" Matt asked when Bolling stopped to light his pipe again.

The old man tamped tobacco into the bowl of his pipe, frowning thoughtfully. Suddenly his face lighted. "Yep. Reckon I do. Name of Sim Carlton. He worked for Preston Jok. He did a good deal of the locating that Jok was supposed to do. Good hand, too. Everybody was well satisfied with his work. As far as I know, he never made a single mistake in getting folks located on the property they wanted."

"What happened to him?"

Bolling sighed. "I wish I knew. I can usually find out things. But Sim just disappeared, and nobody has seen hide nor hair of him since. Guess he got tired of his job and drifted on."

"Doesn't Jok know where he went?"

"Nope. I asked him. He said he was at work one day and the next day he didn't come back. Jok didn't think much about that. But when he didn't show up the next day, Jok went to the hotel where he had a room. All they knew there was that Sim left one night right after supper and never showed up again. Why are you asking?"

"I just heard that a fellow disappeared from here. I wondered about him. I guess he was a friend of Fred's."

Bolling nodded vigorously as if that explained Matt's curiosity. "That's right; he was. About the same age, I'd say. Sim was a little wild, too. Ran around with a tough crowd sometimes. Fred never did that." He squinted at Matt's belt. "Ain't packing a gun, I see.

Can't say as that's such a smart thing to do around here."

"Ever hear of anybody getting shot because he didn't carry a gun?" Matt asked.

Bolling took his pipe from his mouth and pursed his lips. "No, I can't say that I have," he said slowly. "Just the same, if you can use a hogleg, you'd better have one handy. This town is getting ripe for some fireworks. That's the way the compass points."

Matt looked at his watch. Almost noon. He rose and moved to the door. "I suppose these settlers around here have a sort of leader, don't they?" he asked.

Bolling nodded. "Walt Jensen is their big wheel. He's a quiet fellow, doesn't say much and doesn't get riled very easy. The only reason I can see why they all look to him for orders is because he's so big. He'll weigh a third as much as a yearling steer, and he's tall enough so that he doesn't look fat. You'll like him, I reckon."

"Any relation to this Suzy Jensen you were talking about?"

"She's his daughter, and no more like him than the Tumbleweed is to the Red River." He chuckled. "I'll bet if you go out there, Suzy will have you wrapped around her finger, too, inside half an hour."

Matt laughed. "I'd take that bet, but I don't like to rob an old man. Where does Jensen live?"

"Up the creek a couple of miles," Bolling said, jerking his thumb to the west. "Most of the settlers took the bottom land to the east. But Jensen wanted to be alone, I guess. He's a little like that. Yet everybody likes and respects him."

"I think I'll ride up and see him when I get a chance. And I won't come back wrapped around Suzy's finger."

His laugh blended with Bolling's as he left the livery stable.

CHAPTER III

It was noon when Matt got back to the mill. He had eaten and was cleaning up his few dishes when he heard a horse outside.

He glanced through the window, but all he could see were the hind quarters of a skinny sorrel horse. Moving to the door, he opened it and faced his visitor, a sallow-cheeked, thin boy that Matt quickly guessed to be in his early teens.

The boy's voice quivered with nervousness when he spoke. "Are you Fred Freeman's. brother?"

Matt nodded. "That's right. Come in."

He stepped back and the boy shuffled in, ragged cap in his hand.

"I'm Billy Larabee," he said. "I worked for Fred. I heard this morning that you had come, so I rode in to see if I could do anything."

"That's good of you, Billy," Matt said, thinking he was going to like this boy. "I guess there isn't much that can be done now. You say you worked for Fred?"

Billy nodded. "I know quite a bit about milling. Fred

showed me. I'm older than I look. Sixteen, going on seventeen. I can do a lot of work."

"I haven't decided yet just what I will do about the mill," Matt said. "But if I open it again, would you like to have your old job back?"

Billy's eyes lighted. "I'll say I would. We need it. Papa isn't able to do much work. And Mama can't do enough to make a living for all of us."

"How many in your family, Billy?"

"Just the four of us. Papa, Mama, Tillie and me. But Tillie's only seven and she's crippled."

Matt studied the boy for a minute.

"Where do you live?" he asked.

"About a mile east of town. Papa homesteaded a quarter of land there. It's good land, but it's pretty hard for us to farm it. As soon as spring comes, I'll have to help there. But I can work here till then. I'll work hard."

Matt smiled at the eagerness of the boy. "All right, Billy. You've got a job if I open the mill again."

"You've just got to open it," Billy said earnestly. "Papa says if the mill closed, we'd all have to leave."

"Maybe I'll come down and talk to your father," Matt said.

Billy smiled. "I wish you would."

"I'll come down this afternoon after the funeral."

Billy's face sobered. "I'd like to go to the funeral, but I don't have any nice clothes."

Matt laid a hand on the boy's head. "You're dressed well enough, Billy. Fred never objected to the way you dressed when you worked for him, did he?"

Billy shook his head.

"Then he'd want you to come to the funeral just like you are."

The little church was full when Mark Tuttle, the minister, stood up behind the pulpit and spoke to the congregation.

Matt glanced from Billy, who was sitting slumped in his seat, head bowed against his chest, unashamed tears on his face, to other solemn faces around the room. Just behind Billy was a man Matt took to be Billy's father.

Back in the corner of the room was a huge man with a big round face and sky blue eyes. Walt Jensen, Matt guessed from Bolling's description of the farmer. And with Jensen was a tall shapely girl. Matt couldn't resist a second look. Her hair was a silver blonde and her eyes the same sky blue as those of the man beside her.

Matt only half heard the words the preacher was saying as he stole glances back at the rest of the crowd.

Sid Bolling was there, close to the back. Preston Jok was only a row behind Matt, and the marshal, Pete Guckert, was with him. There were several more, farmers mostly, that Matt didn't know and couldn't recognize from the meager descriptions Bolling had given him.

But one man back close to the door gave Matt a start. He certainly hadn't expected to see Bullard Sanford here.

Then the preacher finished his sermon and six men, hats in hand, lifted the casket and carried it out to a waiting wagon. The cemetery was on a hill just south of town. From the hill, Matt could see the town and most of the valley spread out below him. Several sod houses dotted the flat land below town, and one solitary soddy stood along the creek bank to the west. A wagon road ran to the west of the cemetery and disappeared in the hills to the southwest. The road to Sanford's Broken S Ranch, Matt guessed.

Most of the folks at the church had followed the hearse out to the cemetery in rigs or on foot, and they stood around the grave now, the men with their hats in their hands, while the preacher gave another short eulogy.

Then it was over and most of the people were gone. Matt stood looking over the valley.

The minister stopped beside him. "Shall we go back to town, Mr. Freeman?" he suggested.

Matt nodded. "I reckon. There's nothing more we can do here."

Matt found Billy waiting for him at the mill. "Papa went on home," he said, "but I wanted to wait for you."

Matt had already decided it would be best to talk to Walt Jensen before he confronted Billy's father. "You'd better go on home, Billy," he said. "I've got to ride out to Jensen's; then I'll come out to your place."

Billy nodded, showing only slight disappointment. "All right. Papa would have waited for you, but he had some fence he had to fix. Mama was trying to do it herself while Papa came to the funeral."

"You run along then and help him," Matt said. "I'll be out later."

He went inside as Billy urged his horse into a rough trot up the slope. Going to the shed, Matt saddled his horse, leading him out and down to the creek below the dam to water. When he got back to the mill, he discovered he had company. Falley, the hardware owner, was standing by the mill door, two gun belts in his hand.

"I missed you uptown," Falley explained. "These were Fred's gun belts. I wanted to give them to you. You might have need for them."

Matt took the belts. "Thanks, Falley. It's nice to have them but I don't expect to use them."

"You mean you don't intend to wear any guns?"

Matt nodded. "That's right."

Falley shifted his feet and turned away.

Before Matt could take the guns inside, a rider came down the road, swinging out around Falley and reining in before Matt. Bull Sanford's black brows pulled together as he saw the gun belts Matt was holding.

"I wanted to talk business with you a minute, Freeman," Sanford announced.

"A minute's all I've got," Matt said. "What's on your mind?"

"Well, I hear you fell heir to this mill, and I don't suppose you know anything about milling, so you'd probably like to get rid of it."

"I know a little about milling," Matt said. "Who wants to buy it?"

"I do," Sanford said. "I can't give you a lot, but it's more than you can get from anybody else."

"Last night you wanted to burn it. Now you want to buy it. Why the change in plans?"

Sanford frowned, but his tone of voice didn't change. "I'll probably still burn it. I sure don't intend to run it. I'm just giving you a chance to make some money on the deal. You won't make anything if you keep it, that's sure."

"What makes you so sure of that?"

Sanford's face pulled down in a scowl. "Take my word for it, Freeman: there's no money in milling in Tumbleweed."

"Any reason why it should be a poor business here when it's a good business any other place?"

"There's a good reason why," Sanford said. "And I don't figure you're so dumb you can't see it. I'll give you five hundred dollars for the mill, lock, stock and barrel. How about it?"

"I'll have to think about it," Matt said slowly. "You might not make good enough flour for the settlers."

Sanford swore. "I'd put gunpowder in it."

Matt grinned. "That's what I figured. I'm not going to sell till I look the situation over, Sanford. But I'll rest your mind a little. I haven't decided yet to reopen the mill."

Sanford pushed back his hat. "If you're smart, you

won't ever open it." He wheeled his horse and dug in his spurs.

CHAPTER IV

After returning from the Larabee's, Matt watered his horse and stabled him in the shed by the mill. Darkness had settled down when he opened the door and went into his one-room living quarters. He closed the door, then picked up the lantern and leaned toward the stove to strike a match. Suddenly he froze in that leaning position as a voice behind him ordered:

"Don't light it."

For a moment Matt froze; then he slowly straightened and set the lantern back on the table.

"Don't turn around."

Matt stopped in the act of turning his head. "You're making it a little tough to carry on a conversation," he said.

"You just answer questions," the voice snapped. "And keep facing the other way."

Matt was trying to identify the voice. He was certain that he had heard it before.

"What if I decide I want a look at your face?" Matt asked, determined to make the intruder talk.

"It will be the last thing you'll ever see," the man warned.

Matt still couldn't tie that voice to any man he had seen in Tumbleweed. "I doubt if your face is pretty enough to be worth that," he said.

"Shut up," the man growled. "Where's that box?"

A chill ran over Matt. Here could be the man who had shot Sim Carlton in a futile effort to get the key to the box.

"What box are you talking about?" Matt stalled.

"You know what box. Your brother had it."

"What he had was none of my business. He was dead when I got here."

Matt heard the man behind him shuffling back but he didn't move. Only when he heard the door swing shut did he wheel. He was reaching for the door knob when two bullets slammed into the lower part of the door.

Matt dodged to one side and waited. Apparently the man had orders not to let himself be seen, and he was carrying out those orders. Matt rubbed his chin and looked down at the floor where splinters from the door were barely visible in the darkness.

Outside, a horse pounded away, and Matt sighed, picked up his lantern again and lit it. After a while he carried the lantern outside and looked at the tracks the visitor's horse had made, but they told him nothing. He went back inside and cooked his supper.

Sometime in the night he thought he heard a knock on his door, then decided it had been the wind.

But when he opened the door the next morning, he discovered his mistake. A paper pinned to the door with a small knife was rustling in the early dawn breeze. Matt pulled the knife out of the wood and took it and the paper inside. Scratched on the paper was a warning to get out of the country while he still had a whole hide.

Matt fingered the paper idly, looking at the knife. He had never seen it before and wondered where the warning had come from. It could have come from the same man who had visited him last night in the dark. Or it could have come from someone like Gyp Sanford. Gyp wanted him gone. There was no doubt about that. But somehow he couldn't quite make Gyp and his night visitor fit the same pattern. Maybe it was just a hunch, but he didn't believe Gyp was looking for the box. Somebody else was doing that.

Breakfast over, he saddled his horse.

Matt rode down to Larabee's and told Adam Larabee he was calling a meeting of the farmers at the mill the next afternoon. Billy was there, listening attentively.

"Want a job, Billy?" Matt asked.

"You bet," Billy said quickly.

"I'll give you a half dollar to ride down the valley and tell every farmer about the meeting. I'd like to have everyone there."

"I'll tell them," Billy promised.

"I'll ride up and tell Jensen," Matt said. "See you tomorrow, Larabee."

"I'll be there," Adam Larabee said. "And I hope you've got some scheme that will pull us through."

Matt found Walt Jensen mending some harness. While he was explaining the meeting to Jensen, Suzy came out of the house and down to the barn where the men were talking.

"I thought we had company," she said brightly. "I've put on some extra dinner and I won't take no for an answer."

Matt grinned and looked at his watch. It was almost noon. "All right, Miss Jensen, I'll stay."

"And none of that Miss Jensen, either," she said. "I'm just Suzy to everybody."

Matt laughed. "All right, Suzy. But I'm warning you: when you invite a bachelor to dinner, it means a lot of cooking. He just exists between meal invitations."

The girl laughed, made some remark that Matt didn't catch and went back into the house. Matt turned to Jensen.

"Do you think the farmers will like this idea?"

Jensen sighed. "I don't know. I like the sound of it if we can accomplish it without a fight. I'm a peaceable man; I don't like trouble."

"None of us do," Matt said. "But sometimes we have to fight or give up everything we have. It looks like that's what you settlers are facing here."

Jensen rubbed his hands together thoughtfully. "I'm afraid so. But I don't want trouble."

"You'll have to make up your mind before the meeting tomorrow, Jensen," Matt said flatly. "I figure we'll have trouble, all right. I don't think you can stay in this valley without fighting for it. But if you decide you don't want to fight for what's yours and say so tomorrow at the meeting, the rest won't fight, either. And this whole idea will go up in smoke. I'd like to know what I can depend on from you."

"I'll think about it, Matt," the big farmer said slowly. "I don't make up my mind in a hurry, especially where it means a fight. But if I decide to go along with you, I'll stick."

Matt nodded. "I'm sure of that, Walt."

Suzy called them, and Matt washed up and went in to dinner with Jensen.

Matt found himself thinking about Suzy Jensen more than he was of the coming meeting when he finally left the homestead late in the afternoon and started back to town.

Suzy wasn't just pretty, he decided. She was beautiful. Then he thought of Billy Larabee's comparison of Suzy and Jennie Kent. "Sure she's pretty," Billy had said, "but not half as pretty as Jennie." Matt laughed aloud. Billy was completely infatuated with the teacher. She was probably the first girl he had ever considered as anything but a nuisance.

Matt looked up when he heard a horse coming along the trail ahead of him. He was surprised to find that he was almost back to town and his horse had held to the main trail instead of cutting off toward the mill.

A little shock ran over him as he recognized the rider. He had been thinking about Jennie Kent and now he was coming face to face with her. He reined up and waited. She pulled her horse down to a walk as she approached.

"Hello, Miss Kent," Matt said, touching his hat.

She stopped her horse. "Hello." She looked at him

closely; then her eyes began to sparkle. "I believe we met before under slightly different circumstances."

"Quite different," he said. "Your day's work is done, I suppose?"

"Just the obvious part of it. I've got a bundle of papers to correct tonight. Then I have to get ready for tomorrow night's social. You're coming, I suppose?"

"I hadn't heard anything about it. I've been pretty busy, and it hasn't been with socials."

Her face clouded. "I understand. But our social gatherings are for the general welfare of the entire community," she went on lightly. "It helps to build good will."

He grinned. "This country could use some of that, I reckon. Where is it to be?"

"At the schoolhouse. We usually have it on Friday night, but this time it was postponed to Saturday night."

She didn't offer any explanation for the postponement and he didn't ask. He could tell by her face that this social meant a lot to her; it was probably her own idea.

"What happens at the social?" he asked.

"Everyone has a good time," she said. "We have a short program, games, and tomorrow night we have a box supper."

He grinned. "I think I'd like that. A bachelor always welcomes some good cooking."

He nudged his horse on toward town.

CHAPTER V

Matt had the meeting at the mill set for two o'clock Saturday afternoon. Through the morning, he planned how he would get his idea across to skeptical farmers in a way to convince them.

He went uptown a while before noon to invite Preston Jok down to the meeting. It had been Jok who had saved the mill from being burned the night Matt got to town. He seemed to have the interest of the settlers at heart.

Jok seemed very pleased at Matt's invitation and promised to be on hand.

"I want to see the settlers make a go of it," he told Matt. "I've located them on the best land along the creek. If they fail, it will be a reflection on me."

Matt crossed the street to the marshal's office and found the lawman dozing in a chair behind an old battered desk. The jail in the back of the building was empty, the door of its one cell standing open. Pete Guckert roused from his nap when he heard Matt come through the door.

"Howdy, Freeman," he said, yawning. "Something on your mind?"

Matt leaned against the door jamb. "I was wondering why you didn't arrest Gyp Sanford the day he killed Fred. There seems to be no doubt he was the one who killed Fred."

"I know he was the one," Guckert said. "I saw the

whole thing. But I didn't have a chance to stop it. Lots of other people saw it, too. That's why I didn't arrest Gyp. A dozen people were right there and swore it was an even draw. You can't arrest a man in a case like that."

Matt nodded. "I guess you're right, Guckert. I just wanted to be sure. There's usually a hearing, I thought."

"I reckon you could call our meeting out there in the street after the fight a hearing. I have a list of the witnesses who swore to the even draw. Want to see it?"

Matt sighed. "I guess not." He turned toward the door. "I hope there isn't any more killing."

"So do I." Guckert settled back in his chair. "This marshal job is all right as long as they don't stir up any ruckus like that."

Matt went back down the slope to the mill. He evidently had no grounds for a complaint against Gyp Sanford. But he still suspected that Fred had been prodded into that fight just so Sanford, a fast gunman, could get rid of him. If he was right in that guess, then Matt might be the next one to be sucked in if he allowed it. Well, they'd have to think up something new, for he wore no guns and he didn't intend to.

The settlers began coming early, and by two the space in front of the loading platform was milling with the fifteen or more men who had responded to Matt's call. Matt recognized most of the men. But Billy Larabee had brought some up from down the creek that Matt had never seen before. Jok was there and so was Sid Bolling.

Matt stepped up on the platform. "Most of you have an idea why I invited you here," he began. "Now I want to give you the details of my plan. If it works you'll all make money. But it will take your cooperation. I intend to take out these stone burs and put in rollers."

"Why?" one farmer demanded, scowling. "These burs make good flour."

"The rollers will make better flour," Matt said. "I can sift out the bran from the flour made with the rollers. Your flour will be white with no bran in it, and the bread it makes will be better."

"What's that got to do with us?" another man asked.

Matt began to relax. Those questions showed their interest, and that was all he asked. "You're not getting a fair price for your wheat that you sell at Meadows," he said. "That situation is not liable to change. You need more to live on than just grain for your stock and bread for your table. You need money from the crops you raise. You can make that money by grinding your wheat into flour with rollers and selling the flour."

"Who to?" Adam Larabee asked.

"To the merchants in Meadows. My guess is that somebody who wants you out of this valley has bribed the elevator man in Meadows. But they can't bribe all the merchants. Once the women in and around Meadows find out what kind of bread they can bake with this new flour, they'll buy it and you'll have a market for your wheat."

"Who's going to convince them your roller-made

flour will make better bread?"

"I've got that figured, too," Matt said. "As soon as I get the rollers installed, I'll grind some flour out of the wheat in the bin now, and we'll throw a big celebration and invite all the merchants and everybody around Meadows and give them free samples of the bread made from this flour. That will convince them."

"You're mighty sure that bread will be better, ain't you?" said a skeptical man from the rear of the crowd.

"Mighty sure," Matt said. "I've eaten it myself and I know."

Heads began to nod as the idea took root. "But just how do we figure to make so much?" someone asked.

"We'll grind your wheat and sell flour instead of wheat," Matt explained. "I'll make my profit from grinding and you will get the rest. I figure we ought to get the equivalent of a dollar a bushel for your wheat when it's ground into flour."

One man whistled. "I'd be rich in a year or two of that. I can plant a lot of wheat on my quarter."

"That's where I need your cooperation," Matt said. "I want you to put out all the wheat you can after you've planted what feed and corn you need."

One farmer, a big man with a stubbly beard, pushed to the front of the group. "We know we're getting robbed in Meadows. We've tried a time or two to haul our wheat on to Prairie Bend. But something happens every time so we don't get there. What's going to keep something from happening to our loads of flour we take to Meadows?"

"That is a problem," Matt admitted. "But it's only eighteen miles. We can protect our loads that far. If things start happening, we'll use guards."

"That will mean a fight," one man said, shaking his head. "I don't like that."

Sid Bolling's shrill voice piped up for the first time in the meeting. "It's fight or starve, Sam. You ought to know that. So far they've been content to let you starve slowly. But if they find they can lick you that easy, the time will come when they'll take after you and run you clean out of the country."

A few heads nodded in agreement. Matt looked over the men. "It may not come to trouble. I hope not. Maybe when they see we're working our way around them, they'll give up. If they don't, it's like Sid said. We'll have to fight or starve."

"If we're going to have to fight anyway, we could take a guard and haul our wheat to Prairie Bend," one man said tentatively.

"That's right," Matt said. "But you've got twice as far to haul your wheat and you'd be gone twice as long from your homes. And the going between Meadows and Prairie Bend would be a lot rougher. Too many places for ambushes. It's not like that between here and Meadows."

The big man in the front began to nod his head slowly. "Sounds good," he repeated. "We've sure got to do something. What do you say, Walt?"

Matt almost held his breath. He knew if the farmers were to be convinced, Walt Jensen would have to sanction it. Now the question had been put squarely to the big Norwegian, and Matt watched for his reaction.

As usual, Jensen was slow in replying. "I'd do almost anything to keep out of a fight," he said finally. "I've been thinking this over ever since Matt told me about it yesterday. I've about decided the same as Sid has. If we keep laying down and playing dead dog, they're going to get braver and end up by running us right out of the valley. I ain't about to be pushed off my claim. I'm voting to go along with Matt's idea. We ain't got a thing to lose."

Matt breathed easier. As he had expected, Jensen's opinion swung the balance. Within a minute, every man there was voting for Matt's scheme.

"I'll go after the rollers as soon as possible," Matt promised. "Now it's up to you to plant what wheat you can."

"We'll plant a lot," Jensen promised. "We haven't got time now to break more ground, but we'll seed what we have. We'll start next week."

Sid Bolling was the last to leave. "We'll see now what Bull and Gyp Sanford do about this," he said speculatively as he headed up the slope. . . .

That evening Matt donned his best clothes and headed straight south up the slope to the schoolhouse.

Rigs and a few saddle horses lined the front of the building and the south side. It looked as if a big crowd were on hand. Matt went inside and stopped close to the door, feeling as though he didn't belong here. This was a community affair, and he wasn't sure he had been here long enough to be accepted as part of the community.

He saw many of the men who had been at his meeting this afternoon; they had their families with them now. And the Sanfords were here, Bull and Gyp and a small black-haired woman Matt guessed to be Bull's wife. There was one unfamiliar face that caught Matt's eye. Maybe it was because of the clothes the man was wearing. He was a medium-sized fellow with a neatly pressed brown suit that stood out in sharp contrast to the clean and sometimes patched overalls and Levis.

Another family came in, the girls and women hiding boxes under loosely wrapped papers and giggling self-consciously as everyone watched them push up to the front and hand their boxes to the teacher. The boys, both old and young, tried playfully to get a look at the boxes under the papers.

Then the entertainment started and Matt was amazed at the talent that came to the front of the room to present itself. He clapped hardest, though, for crippled little Tillie Larabee, who limped to the front of the room and played a tune, breathy but recognizable, on the jew's-harp.

Then it was time for the box social, and Jennie took charge, first thanking those who had helped with the program.

"All you men who want to buy boxes, come over and pay Mrs. Meade twenty-five cents," Jennie said. "She'll give you a number, and Mrs. Tuttle over on this side will give you the box with the same number."

Before any of the men started for the chair where Mrs. Meade waited, somebody spoke up, halting all action.

"Introduce us to the new doc, Jennie. You never know when we might need him."

Jennie laughed and motioned for the man in the brown suit to stand.

"This is Doctor Curt Henley," she said clearly. "He came in on the hack today and will be open for business in his new office on Monday."

Henley smiled and bowed to the crowd, then sat back down as the men began to work their way toward Mrs. Meade. Matt took a closer look at Curt Henley. He was a clean-cut young fellow and, though he looked completely out of place, Matt guessed from the square line of his jaw that he had good stuff in him.

Matt held back, debating whether he should get in line and buy a box. If there weren't enough to go around, he'd better not get one. Then he noticed Billy Larabee standing just on the other side of the door, watching the men longingly.

"What's wrong, Billy?" Matt asked, moving over. "Afraid somebody else will get your girl's box?"

While he talked he fished a quarter out of his pocket and slipped it surreptitiously into Billy's pocket.

"I know they will. I had to spend my money for a fork handle."

"You must have a quarter left," Matt said.

"If I did have, I'd be up there getting my box," Billy

said. "I ain't got a lot of money like most fellows."

Matt detected the bitterness of thwarted youth in Billy's voice.

"Surely you didn't spend all your money, Billy," Matt said. "Better check your pockets again and see."

"I guess I know what I've got," Billy said bitterly. Nevertheless, his hand strayed into his pocket. His eyes widened in surprise, and he jerked his hand out and stared at the quarter in disbelief.

"Never want to take things for granted, Billy," Matt said.

"That's your quarter," Billy accused him. "You put it there."

"It's not mine," Matt denied. "Now come on. Let's get in line or we won't get a box."

His face beaming, Billy stepped up to the line, and Matt took up a station behind him. Glancing at the stack of boxes, Matt decided there would be plenty for all who wanted one. Several men were slipping quietly out the door. Men who couldn't afford to spend a quarter, Matt decided, and didn't want to be embarrassed by sitting alone while others ate their suppers.

Matt thought he would be the last man to draw a number, but he felt rather than saw another man behind him and turned. Doctor Curt Henley had left his seat and fallen in line.

"The last man has as good a chance of being lucky as the first," Henley said, smiling a little at Matt.

Matt nodded knowingly, glancing at Jennie. "Some people are just born lucky. Anyway, you'll get to eat some of the grub they have around here and you'll know what you're up against as a doctor."

"Looks like a healthy lot of people to me," Henley said, looking over the room.

"Physically most of them are. If they just keep their minds healthy you won't be too busy."

Matt turned back in time to see Gyp taking his number across the room to Mrs. Tuttle. He watched and saw a scowl cloud his face as he looked at the name on the box he was handed in exchange for his number. Matt glanced over the room. Suzy Jensen was sitting close to Mrs. Tuttle, and Matt guessed Gyp had hoped to get her box. He couldn't quite read the expression on Suzy's face. He guessed that her box hadn't been taken yet, for now she was watching the next man as he crossed to Mrs. Tuttle.

Then Billy bought his number and Matt laid down his quarter. He followed Billy across to Mrs. Tuttle and claimed his box. Before he looked at the name, he heard Billy exclaim behind him.

"Dad-burn!"

Matt turned.

"What's wrong, Billy?"

"Look who I got! Tillie!"

Matt found it hard not to laugh. "What's wrong with eating with your sister?"

"I eat her grub every day."

Billy started off toward his sister, and Matt opened the box he had gotten. The name fairly jumped at him. Jennie Kent. Henley was standing close to him, opening his box. Matt glanced at him. He had the box Henley wanted. Henley was lifting a name card off the top of the food in his box.

"Know her?" he asked, showing Matt a card that read: "Suzy Jensen."

"I sure do," Matt said, glancing around at Suzy. Apparently she hadn't discovered that her box had been drawn.

Matt showed Henley his name card. "Want to trade?"

Henley's eyes glistened in the light of the kerosene lamps. "Is it permissible?"

"Mrs. Tuttle and Jennie are the only ones who know whose boxes we drew. They won't object."

"Don't you want Jennie's box?"

"I didn't say that," Matt said quickly. "You're a stranger here, so I'll give you a break. But next time I draw Jennie, you'll be out of luck."

The doctor laughed softly. "You and I should be friends. Maybe I can do you a favor sometime."

CHAPTER VI

Gyp Sanford was leaning against the hitchrack, a cigarette dangling from his lips, when Matt first saw him the next morning as he came out of church. Gyp came erect, flipping away the cigarette, the second Matt walked through the door.

"Freeman," he snapped, "I've got something to say to you."

Matt moved to one side of the doorway so no one would be behind him. "Say it." His voice matched Gyp's curt tone.

"This country ain't big enough for you and me both. Move on."

"I'm not moving, Sanford."

Rage swept over Gyp's face. "Fill your hand," he bellowed, and clawed his gun out of its holster.

Matt didn't move. Here was the test. If Gyp had any reason left, he wouldn't use his gun. For he'd never get out of town alive if he did. These people had just come from church, but they'd go to a lynching within the hour if Gyp shot Matt now.

Apparently a shred of reason still clung in the back of Gyp's brain for, though the hand holding the gun seemed to twitch, the trigger didn't move.

"Yellow belly!" Gyp cried. "Afraid to carry a gun. A sneaking coyote would be ashamed to be seen with you."

Then Gyp's gun roared, the bullet kicking a spray of dust over Matt's boot. Matt didn't move, and Gyp slapped another bullet an inch closer.

"Dance, you yellow belly!" Gyp roared, and squeezed the trigger again.

Still Matt didn't move, and twice more the gun roared. The last bullet clipped the heel off one boot. The sudden jolt threw Matt off balance and he sprawled in the dirt. Screams went up from the women watching, but Matt came to his feet in one bound.

He had kept count. Five shots Gyp had squeezed off. Unless he was a reckless man with a gun, he never kept a cartridge under the hammer when his gun was in the holster. That left him just five shots.

At any other time, Matt might have played it safe and held back. But his restraint was worn paper thin. A desire to get at the man and tear him limb from limb was overpowering him.

He started walking toward Gyp, limping on the foot without any boot heel. Surprise held Gyp motionless for a moment, and he stared at Matt in disbelief. Matt came closer until he was within ten feet before Gyp jarred himself into action.

He squeezed the trigger again, and this time he wasn't aiming at Matt's feet. But the hammer fell on an empty cylinder. With an oath, he threw the gun straight at Matt's head. But Matt had been expecting just such a move and ducked, letting the gun flash over his shoulder. Then he charged forward, still in his crouch.

Gyp didn't give ground. Instead, he met Matt's charge with a bellow, fists swinging. He was fifteen pounds heavier than Matt but a couple of inches shorter, and his arms didn't have the reach that Matt's had.

After a vicious exchange of blows, Matt backed off a couple of steps and met every advance of Gyp's with stinging jabs that brought the blood out on Gyp's face and curses to his lips.

Then, as he tried to sidestep one of Gyp's charges,

the heeless boot tripped him. Gyp twisted suddenly and fell on him. In spite of the extra weight, Matt was still holding his own when he felt the heavier man lunge sideways. He twisted his head just in time to see the barrel of the gun swinging toward his head.

The crowd was gone when Matt opened his eyes again. He was on a cot in a room that was so new it still smelled of pine pitch and paint. His head was throbbing, and for a moment he couldn't quite remember what had happened. Then it flooded back into his memory.

"How's your head?" someone asked.

Matt looked up at Jennie. "Like a barrel with rocks in it," he said. "I don't recognize this place."

"This is my office," Henley said from the foot of the cot. "We didn't want to leave you out in the sun till you came around. That was quite a wallop he gave you."

Matt touched his head. "It doesn't take a doctor to convince me of that. Tell me something I don't know."

Henley smiled at Jennie. "I guess he'll pull through all right." He looked back at Matt. "You'd better rest for an hour or two; then I think you'll be as good as new except for a headache and a boot with no heel."

Matt looked at his watch and saw that he had been out only a few minutes. He relaxed again, and slept.

When he awoke this time he felt much better, though his head still ached and was as sore as a boil. He was amazed to find it was nearly three o'clock. He got up and went out to the front room of the little office. On the desk he found a key with a note telling him to lock the door and bring the key to the hotel.

After delivering the key to the hotel desk for Henley, he went up to the hotel, asked for Jok's room number and went to it. Pete Guckert came out just as Matt was ready to knock. He merely nodded as though he barely saw him and went on down the hall while Jok invited Matt inside.

"Where was Guckert this morning when Gyp Sanford was showing off?" Matt asked.

"I don't know," Jok said easily. "But there wasn't much he could have done, anyway. There's no law in Tumbleweed against carrying a gun."

"There ought to be a law against shooting at people."

"But he didn't hit you."

"I'll bet he could dig up a law against it if I was fanning the lead around his heels."

Jok laughed. "I imagine he'd look all right. But you did yourself proud this morning, Freeman. Really put yourself in solid with the homesteaders. That support can come in handy."

"I reckon," Matt said, "although I hadn't thought about it that way."

He looked at the lawyer, studying the man. He was as well groomed as if he'd just stepped out of a tailor's shop. His hair was neatly combed and his boots freshly polished. But his thoughts were deeply hidden behind the faint smile that he kept on his face most of the time.

"Now what can I do for you, Freeman?" Jok asked, lounging back in a chair.

Matt outlined briefly what he needed at the mill. "I figure it will take in the neighborhood of three thousand dollars to buy the stands of rollers, belts, sieves, and lumber to make the chutes and elevator. And I'll have to hire at least one carpenter to oversee the work of making those chutes."

After Matt had finished Jok sat rubbing his chin silently. Finally he nodded. "For the good of the community, I want to see you make a success here. I'll put up the money against a first mortgage on the mill. We'll make the terms of payment easy on you."

"The mill should be good security."

"That's right. But I don't ever want to foreclose. Can you imagine what I'd do with a flour mill?"

Matt couldn't keep from joining in the lawyer's laughter. Jok running a mill would be a sight to behold, all right.

It was nearly supper time when Matt went down the slope to the mill. He was satisfied with his accomplishment. Tomorrow he would go to McCook and order the rollers for the mill. With good luck, in three months he should be ready to start grinding flour with the rollers.

He had supper almost ready when he heard a knock at the door. Caution gripped him and he picked up the rifle, holding it in one hand while he opened the door with the other. What he saw there made him forget his caution.

A small man, well past middle age, was leaning against the door jamb. Blood streaked his swollen face and he appeared about ready to drop. Matt set his rifle down and stepped out to help the man inside.

"I've got to rest," the man murmured.

Matt sat him in a chair and closed the door. "You can rest there awhile. I'll get some water and see what I can do."

The man passed out while Matt washed his face and put some salve, which he found on the top shelf of the cupboard, on the cuts on his face. One cut, just over the man's left eye, was very deep, and Matt guessed it might have caused some damage to that eye. His clothes were torn until they barely clung to him.

When he finished cleaning up the man's face and doctoring the cuts, Matt put him on the cot. Then he debated going for Doctor Henley. The man opened his eyes and looked around, seeming to read Matt's mind.

"Don't call a doc," he whispered.

"What happened to you?" Matt asked, deciding against going for the doctor immediately.

"Got beat up," the man said weakly. "Tried to get out of town. Couldn't make it, so I stopped here."

"Who did it?"

The man's right eye brightened. "I don't know," he said.

Matt was sure he was lying.

"What's your name?" Matt asked.

"Just call me John," the man said, his voice stronger now.

"Don't you have any other name?"

The man nodded weakly. "I've got one. But I was kicked out of my home when I was a kid. I've never used that name since." He paused for breath. "I'm just John."

Matt nodded.

"I'll be getting out of your way as soon as I can," John went on. "I would like to spend the night here."

Matt nodded. "No reason why you can't."

The man managed a weak smile. "Maybe I can do you a favor some day." Worry came back to his face. "There seems to be something in my left eye."

Matt looked closer. "I'll take a look," he said. "I'll have to hold my hand over your other eye."

He placed a hand tightly over John's right eye, then passed the other hand back and forth just above the left. The eye didn't flicker.

"See anything?" he asked.

John shook his head. Matt knew then. The sight was completely gone in that eye.

"You'll have to wear a patch over that eye for a while till it gets better," he said.

"Blind in one eye, ain't I?" John said heavily. "But I'll look different with a patch over one eye, I guess."

Matt thought he detected a note of shrewdness mingled with the despair in the man's tone.

CHAPTER VII

Billy Larabee rode down to the mill the next morning before Matt was ready to start for McCook. Eagerness brightened his thin face as he slid off his horse and hurried into the mill.

"Papa says I should watch your mill for you while you're gone," he said, then stopped short as he saw John leaning his chair against the wall behind the table. "I didn't know you had company."

"Just a fellow passing through," Matt said. "He stayed with me last night."

John nodded, the dark patch over his left eye making a splotch on his pale face. He was still weak, so weak Matt didn't want to start him on the road again.

"Is he going to watch your mill for you?" Billy asked.

"I hadn't thought about that," Matt said, thinking of the new problem John's presence had created.

"I'll need help at it, I reckon," John said. "I can't see everything with only one eye. Might even need someone to watch me." He glanced at Matt.

Matt was silent for a minute. He liked John and felt he could trust him. But he really didn't know the man or the motives that drove him. Yet what choice did he have? He had to go to McCook to order the machinery for the mill, and he couldn't turn John out in his weakened condition.

"Might be a good idea for you both to stay if you want the job."

"I've got no objection," John said. "I like to have a bed to sleep in. But I don't know much about milling. Better put the boy in charge. If anybody tries any dirty work, he'll be more apt to know."

"How about it, Billy?" Matt asked.

"Sure," Billy said eagerly. "Papa says the farmers here can't afford to let anything happen to the mill now."

"He's right about that. I'm ready to hit the road now. I'll try to be back tomorrow."

John leaned forward, resting his elbows on the table. "How about your hardware?"

"I don't carry a gun," Matt said.

A frown tugged at John's forehead. "From what I hear, you had a ruckus yesterday morning down at the church. I wouldn't be wandering around on the prairie without a gun now if I were you."

Matt considered the man's advice for a moment, then shook his head. "I put my guns away six months ago. I didn't even bring them out here with me."

"Fred's are hanging there behind the door," Billy said.

"That's a good place for them," Matt said, and went outside.

Maybe he was nursing his determination to the point of stubbornness. But he had resolved not to take up a gun again unless it was forced on him. If he'd been carrying a gun yesterday morning, somebody would have been killed down at the church. He had avoided it then. But how long could he keep avoiding it? He

60

doubted if Gyp Sanford and he could both stay in the same country much longer.

It was a hard day's ride to McCook, and both Matt and his horse were bone weary when they came in sight of the town built on the steep slopes that climbed up from the north bank of the Republican River. Matt put up his horse in the first livery barn he came to and headed for the hotel. In the morning he'd send out his order, but right now he wanted a hot supper and a warm bed.

He was just in time for the steaming hot supper in the hotel dining room. He found a place at the table and fell in with a dozen and a half other men. Matt guessed most of them were workers, probably at the railroad yards down at the south end of town.

His meal finished, he was just paying his quarter when he caught a glimpse of a man at the door that snapped his head around. The man was dodging out of sight, but Matt was sure he had recognized the blocky build and dark face of Gyp Sanford.

Running to the door, he charged into the street, eyes flashing up and down the sidewalk. A half-dozen men were moving along the street, but at first Matt saw no one who resembled Gyp. Then he saw a heavy-set man running north up the steep slope, and he started after him. If Gyp Sanford were in McCook, there was nothing Matt could do about it. But he wanted to know.

Matt gained on the other man, but it was getting too dark to identify him positively. Then suddenly the man wheeled, and Matt saw the gun in his hand. He dived into a doorway as a bullet ripped into the casing only inches from his head. He waited a minute, but no other shot came; and when he looked out, the street was deserted.

He didn't try to follow the man any farther.

Matt went back to the hotel, moving cautiously. If he were shot down here in the streets of McCook, it would be hard to pin the crime on a man back at Tumbleweed. Maybe Gyp had considered that very thing when he followed him here. He wished he had taken John's advice and strapped on his brother's guns this morning. Being shot at with no chance to shoot back didn't set well with him.

He marveled at the nonchalance of the town. Surely somebody had heard that shot, yet there were no questions and apparently no curiosity among those he met.

He started to sign the hotel register, then suddenly checked the pen. His name and room number in the register would be an open invitation to any man who wanted to catch him asleep. He entered the name of Jim Ashton and gave his address as Kansas City. At least Gyp would have to guess.

But his sleep was uninterrupted, and he saw no sign of Gyp Sanford the next morning while he went about his business. He had to send a telegram to Chicago for the rollers. The man at the depot estimated the rollers would be in McCook in ten days.

Matt made arrangements with a freighting company to haul the rollers out to Tumbleweed a week from the next Friday and Saturday. It would take two days for the loaded wagons to make the trip. And they would be big days.

"We can start as soon as the stuff comes," one freighter said.

Matt shook his head. "I want you to start on Friday. I'll meet you that night somewhere this side of Prairie Bend."

"Expecting trouble?"

"It's always a possibility," Matt said. "I'll ride in with you from there on."

"All right by me," the freighter said. "But it won't make it any cheaper."

"I'm not trying to save money. Just my freight. See you a week from Friday."

Matt pushed his horse on the way home. He didn't want to be too late getting back to Tumbleweed.

The late March night settled over the prairie more than an hour before Matt put his horse into the shed by the mill. There was a light in the living quarters, and Matt found both John and Billy there waiting for him.

"We thought you never were coming," Billy exclaimed excitedly.

Matt glanced quickly over the room. Things were scattered everywhere, and only a semblance of order had been restored. John sat slumped in a chair by the table, and his face was as pale as death.

"What happened here?" Matt demanded.

"Somebody tore up the place," Billy said, gulping down his excitement. "I went home to help Papa with the chores, and when I got back John was tied to his chair and only half conscious."

Matt wheeled on John. "What happened?"

John shook his head weakly. "I'm not sure. Just about dark somebody opened the door. I heard the voice and turned. Then something socked me on the head." He rubbed a hand over his head. "I'm really getting a sore head now. When I came to, Billy was here and I was tied in this chair."

"Somebody was looking for something," Billy said. "What do you suppose it was?"

"Hard to tell," Matt said evasively. But in his own mind it wasn't hard to tell at all. Somebody was looking for that box. His hand automatically strayed to his pocket. The key was still there. But he was no better off than the searchers, for he didn't know where the box was, either.

He lit a lantern and crossed into the main part of the mill. Things were scattered here, too. Whoever had been here had given the whole mill a good going-over.

"Want me to ride home with you, Billy?" Matt asked when he got back to the living quarters.

"I'll just stay here tonight, if it's all right with you. Papa isn't looking for me home. He didn't think you would get back till tomorrow."

"Sure you can stay," Matt said. It suited him better than a night ride for either him or Billy right now.

Before blowing out the light, Matt took down one of Fred's guns and checked it, then put it under his pillow. The time had come, it seemed, when a gun was more of a comfort than a liability.

Matt left John and Billy in charge of the mill when he rode toward Meadows several days later.

He found the two freight wagons a few miles east of Prairie Bend. They were just pulling up to camp for the night. The driver of the front wagon was a wiry little man with more hair in his moustache than there was on his head.

"Figured you'd be showing up about now," he said. "Still looking for trouble?"

"Looking for it is the best way to avoid it," Matt said. He lifted a corner of the heavy canvas that covered the wagon. "Think I'll sleep in the wagon tonight under this cover."

"Suit yourself," the driver said. "I'll bunk underneath."

Matt didn't really look for trouble, for he didn't see how anyone could know about these wagons unless they had kept an eye on the yards at McCook. He doubted if they had gone to that extreme. Of course, two heavily loaded freight wagons like these, if seen, could rouse people's curiosity in a hurry.

"Somebody want to keep you from putting rollers in your mill?" the freighter asked after supper was over and he was smoking his last pipeful of tobacco before rolling into his blankets.

"Seems that way."

"Don't that beat the dickens?" the little driver murmured. "Every time anyone tries to make a little progress there's always somebody right smack dab in the way trying to stop it. Oh, well, progress generally wins out in the long run."

He and the other driver rolled into their blankets, and Matt worked his way in between two stands of rollers inside the wagon. It wasn't exactly comfortable, but he hadn't come down here just to be comfortable.

He did manage to sleep, and it was some time later when he was roused by a sharp command.

"Hey, you, get out from under those wagons."

Matt didn't move as he heard the driver directly under him swear lustily as he crawled out of his blankets.

"Dump those wagonloads of stuff," the intruder ordered.

Matt lifted the corner of the canvas and peered out. Three riders were lined up just on the other side of the ashes of last night's campfire. Each man had a gun. But they had their faces covered, and it was too dark for Matt to identify anything about them.

"I ain't dumping no wagons," the driver said spiritedly.

"I reckon you will," the spokesman for the three said irritably. "Get to work."

"It took five men to load them," the driver said. "Two of us ain't going to try to unload them."

"Then get out of the way and we'll take care of it."

The driver glanced at the wagon. "We're taking these loads through."

Matt heard the snip of a gun being cocked. His own

66

gun, which he had checked carefully before starting on this trip, came up to the edge of the wagon box and peeked out from under the canvas.

The driver glanced at the wagon again but didn't move. "We're taking them through," he repeated.

Matt watched the raider lift his gun. His own gun was cocked now.

"You heard him," Matt snapped. "We're going through."

A startled exclamation broke from the lips of the leader. His head jerked around wildly.

"Drop your guns," Matt ordered.

But the leader apparently had decided where the voice was coming from. He jerked his gun around. Matt fired then, hitting the man in the hand. The gun went spinning.

"Anybody else want to try it?" he demanded.

The other two dropped their guns and lifted their hands. Then one of them jerked his horse around. "Come on, Dandy," he shouted, and dug in his spurs. The other two followed, the last one holding a bleeding hand and swearing loudly.

Matt crawled out of the wagon. "It probably would be wise for us to hitch up and move on a piece," he said. "They might get more men and come back."

"I wouldn't put it past them," the bald-headed driver said. "But next time they'll get a belly full of lead before they get the drop on me."

Matt picked up the three guns that had been dropped and put them in the wagon. Then they harnessed the horses and moved the wagons up almost to the out-skirts of Prairie Bend. There they bedded down again, but sleep had given way to watchfulness. They wouldn't be caught unaware again.

CHAPTER VIII

There was quite a stir in Tumbleweed when the two freight wagons pulled up to the mill a while before sundown. Half the town came down to watch the unloading, and Matt called for volunteers to help with the work. By dark the machinery was all inside the mill.

As usual where any breeze of excitement was stirring, Sid Bolling was there. Matt asked him to wait around after the others left. Bolling agreed, and when the edge had worn off people's curiosity and they had gone home to supper, he followed Matt inside the living quarters of the mill.

"Can't take long," Bolling said. "This is Saturday night and I'll have plenty of business at the barn."

"What I want to show you won't take long, Sid," Matt said. "We ran into a speck of trouble last night down by Prairie Bend. When it was over, the three men who jumped us ran off without their guns."

Bolling grinned. "On orders, maybe?"

"They were asked politely," Matt said. "I brought their guns home. One has initials on the handle. Do you recognize them?" He held out a gun to the old man.

68

Bolling studied the handle of the gun for a moment. "G. S. That stands for George Sanford. That's Gyp. So he went to guns to stop the rollers from getting here, did he?"

Matt nodded. "I thought it was probably Gyp."

"I know it is," Bolling said. "I'd recognize that gun if there wasn't any initials on it. Who was with him?"

"I don't know. The other guns have no markings on them. But as they were leaving one man called another one Dandy. Does that make sense?"

Bolling whistled. "That fits like a hand in a glove. Dandy Dobson. He runs the elevator in Meadows. He's the one who's been buying what the farmers around here raise. Or rather he's been stealing it. If you put in these rollers and sell flour, it's going to ruin his soft touch. Dandy and Gyp have been thick as thieves lately, I notice."

Matt nodded. "I guess that about tells me what I want to know."

"Any shooting?" Bolling asked.

"I had to convince one of them he was outnumbered."

"Outnumbered? Huh! Hit him?"

"I think I clipped him on the hand. He was the one they called Dandy."

"I'll have a look next time I see Dandy Dobson," Bolling promised. "I've got to get back to the barn now. I see you've finally decided to wear your hardware."

"I needed it on this trip. Probably won't now."

Bolling glared at Matt. "Are you stubborn or just dumb? Every day you stay in this country you're going to need that gun more. After last night, your name will go higher than ever on Gyp's list. Don't step outside without that gun thumping your legs."

Matt thought about that as he went to bed. The old man might be right.

The machinery went into place quickly. But the chutes and elevators took time. Matt had hired a mill expert from Chicago to oversee the construction of the wooden chutes and elevators. With all the help the farmers could give, the work went along rapidly, and Matt was sure the mill would be ready to go by the first of July.

Matt took time off one afternoon late in June to go to Meadows and advertise a big day of celebration he planned in Tumbleweed. He even put a notice of it in the Meadows weekly paper. Everyone around Tumbleweed knew about it already. Matt had set the second Saturday in July as the big day.

The mill was ready to go three days before the celebration. A dozen settlers were on hand when Matt lifted the gate and let the water tumble into the chute and start the big wheel turning. He had some wheat already scoured and tempered ready for the rollers. The men crowded around to watch Matt as he checked the wheat going through the first stand of rollers where it was cracked. Then it moved along to the next set of rollers where it was ground more finely. On it went to even more closely set rollers where it was ground to a powder. On the floor above, Matt could hear the shaking of the sieves as they caught the crushed wheat that was elevated to them from the rollers below and shunted the bran into a chute at one end while the snow-white flour fell through the sieves into another bin.

"There's the flour that will make better bread," Matt said, proudly displaying the contents of the bin. "You've always had bran in your flour before. Couldn't get it out when it was ground with burs. But there's no bran in this."

"Sure looks good," Herb Simpson, the grocer, said. "When do we get to try it?"

"Take some home tonight and let your wife try it," Matt said. "Since we're using the back of your store for a bakery Saturday, she ought to know how this flour will act."

Sid Bolling, who was watching with the others, shook his head. "Makes me hungry just to look at it. Going to take a lot of bread Saturday. Who's going to bake it?"

"I'm calling for volunteers," Matt said. "There are a lot of good cooks, and I think most of them want to help make this a success. We'll have to set the yeast Friday night. We'll bake first thing Saturday morning."

"Suzy has already said she'll come in," Walt Jensen said.

A half-dozen other men promised that their wives or daughters would be in to help. Matt grinned in anticipation. This flour looked wonderful; the wheat from last year's crop had been good. Saturday could be a red letter day for Tumbleweed.

Saturday was a clear day, too warm for comfort. But Matt didn't notice the heat. People from Meadows began arriving by ten o'clock. The cooks had been in the back of Simpson's store since seven. Matt had been there off and on, too. He was a little surprised to see Jennie come in shortly after seven.

"I told you I had an apron," she said gaily, waving it at him as she went into the back room.

Preston Jok came down the street to talk to Matt as the crowd began pouring into town.

"Looks like a real success," the lawyer said, rubbing his hands together. "Now if the bread just proves to be sensational—"

"You still doubt that, don't you, Jok?" Matt said.

"It's hard to believe any revolutionary idea is practical until it is tried. When do the races start?"

"When the folks all get in," Matt said. "It was mighty decent of you to loan me enough money to put up prizes for the races."

Jok smiled easily. "Doesn't take much money to satisfy people like these."

Matt shot a glance at the lawyer, wondering if he had detected a note of condescension in his voice.

There were half a dozen foot races in the forenoon for the youngsters and some for the men and women. Quarters were given as first prizes in the smaller children's races, and half-dollars went to the winners of

72

the races for larger children and grown-ups. But the big race, the one that had helped to draw a crowd, was the horse race to be run after dinner.

Matt was surprised at the size of the crowd as noon drew closer. He hadn't realized there were so many people in the area around Tumbleweed and Meadows. He checked back at the store to see how much bread was baked, and his eyes popped at the long rows of loaves.

"We've got enough," Mrs. Simpson said confidently. "We've got enough butter to spread on every slice, too. Jennie brought some preserves and so did Mrs. Meade. I brought up three quarts from my cellar so we'll have preserves for most of the bread."

Matt grinned. "That's fine. It's about time we started feeding them, I think."

The people had brought their own lunches, but each person, large and small, filed past the front of the store where the women handed out thick slices of warm bread covered with butter and preserves. Matt watched for the reaction, and before a third of the line had gone by, he knew his day was a success. As the line thinned out and the bread still half filled the counter back inside the store, children started pushing into the line for a second helping. And they got it.

"Feed them as long as it lasts," Matt whispered to the serving women. "They're going to beg their folks to buy more flour like this."

It seemed to Matt nothing could go wrong on this day, but that feeling vanished while the crowd was gathering up the remains of their picnic lunches. Two riders came in from the south end of town and left their horses at the hitchrack in front of the blacksmith shop. Matt had hoped Gyp Sanford would stay away from this celebration. But he was here now, too late for the free bread, but in time to cause trouble, Matt guessed. The little fellow with him was a man Matt didn't know.

"Dandy Dobson," Sid Bolling whispered in Matt's ear. Matt wheeled. He hadn't seen Bolling come up.

"Been expecting them two," Bolling said. "Couldn't have a peaceful celebration without Gyp. And Dandy seems to be with him everywhere he goes these days."

"I hear there's going to be a horse race this afternoon," Dobson said loudly to the first man he came to. "Where do I enter my horse?"

"Have to see Matt Freeman," the man said. "There's a lot of horses entered. Better be sure you got a good one. No use running if you ain't."

"I've got a good one, all right," Dobson said confidently.

Matt took a look at the horse Dobson had ridden into town. Anger soared in him. That long-legged roan was obviously a race horse. Dobson was intent on taking the fifteen dollars prize money these homesteaders had been planning and working for. It meant a lot to them. And it meant nothing to Dobson.

"Put my horse, Jigger, down as an entry, Freeman," Dobson said importantly.

"Got it," Matt said, writing the name and owner

down at the bottom of the long list he had. He glanced at Dobson's hand. It had been three months since he had shot the gun out of the man's hand down at Prairie Bend, but the white scar across the back of his hand told the story as clearly as words.

"Want to put up a side bet on any horse in your line against Jigger?" Dobson asked, grinning.

"I'm not making any bets," Matt said shortly.

"Not the sporting kind, eh?"

"I'm not picking the winner," Matt said. "I'm just here to see it's a fair race and that the winner gets the prize."

"You can give me that prize right now and save all this worry about seeing everything is fair."

"Why don't you pull in your horns, Dobson?" Bolling snorted. "You're going to crowd Matt too far some day."

"I'm waiting patiently for that day," Dobson said, his face losing its grin.

"He won't always shoot at your hand," Bolling said significantly.

A stunned silence hit Dobson and Gyp.

Dobson recovered after a minute, and laughed. "Now you've had your joke, how about that bet?"

"I'm not betting," Matt repeated.

"How about odds of ten to one?" Bolling asked suddenly.

Dobson grinned. "Sure. Name your figure."

"I'll tell you what I'll do," Bolling said. "I'll throw ten dollars in the prize kitty and you toss in a hundred.

The winner gets the whole works, one hundred and twenty-five dollars. You'll get it if you win."

Dobson frowned at Bolling for an instant, then nodded. "Fair enough. I'll get it anyway." He dug into his pocket and brought out a hundred dollars in bills. "Now toss in your ten."

Bolling dug out ten dollars. Matt pocketed the extra hundred and ten dollars and, when Dobson and Gyp were gone, turned to the livery man.

"What's the idea, Sid? Didn't you look at his horse down there?"

"Sure I did. And I know he can beat anything entered in the race."

"Then why did you kick in ten dollars?"

"Because I figure on taking Dandy Dobson down a peg or two and also making him poorer by a hundred bucks."

Matt studied the excited gleam in the old man's eyes. "Just how are you figuring on doing that? Shoot his horse, maybe"

Bolling shook his head. "That's an idea, but I'm afraid I'd be too tempted to raise my sights to the rider. I've got a horse down at the barn that can race some. I told you about him. Remember?"

"Do you think that old flea bait can outrun Dobson's horse?"

Bolling started working his way through the crowd toward his livery barn at the end of the street, expecting Matt to follow. "I just kicked in ten dollars that says he can. Will you help me get him ready? We

76

ain't got much time."

"Who's going to ride him?" Matt demanded. "You can't ride any more, and I'm too big."

Bolling nodded as he hurried down the street. "Right on both counts. We've got to find some little fellow. The littler the better."

"Billy Larabee," Matt said suddenly. "He's little and he can handle a horse."

"Get him," Bolling said. "I'll get my horse. Better enter my horse on your sheet there, too. Call him Dynamite."

Billy had entered his old horse in the race when the race had first been announced, but he had reluctantly withdrawn him when the competition had grown too steep for a plowhorse. Matt had found him now and told him what he wanted, and the boy's eyes glowed with excitement.

They met Sid Bolling in front of the livery barn, where he was holding the old horse, whose head drooped as if he were half asleep. Matt found it hard not to laugh when Bolling gave Billy his instructions on how to handle Dynamite.

"He's mighty foxy," Bolling said. "Hold him with a tight rein till you get started; then let him have his head and just hang on. Dynamite will do the rest. By the way, did Matt tell you how much you can win in this race?"

Billy shook his head. "Fifteen dollars, I suppose."

"The prize is one hundred and twenty-five," Bolling said dramatically. "If you win, all I want is my ten dollars back. Could you use a hundred and fifteen?"

Billy's jaw dropped, and when he found his tongue, his voice broke into a childish falsetto. "I'll say!" he squeaked. "Papa needs another horse and some new harness."

"Just remember what I told you," Bolling said. "Watch him close till the race starts; then let him go. Better get over there. Walt is getting ready to start the race."

Matt turned back to the crowded street. Walt Jensen, appointed official starter for the race, was calling all the riders together in preparation to taking them half a mile southeast of town to start the race across the flat bottom land. The race would finish where the road turned into Main Street.

Snickers followed the sway-backed old bay as the contestants rode slowly down the road behind Jensen. Matt saw that Billy's face and neck were red with embarrassment as he sat stiffly on the horse, looking straight ahead. Billy didn't believe the old horse could run, either. Matt confessed to himself he had his doubts, but he was not a total disbeliever. Sid Bolling was sure he could run, and Bolling was a fine judge of horseflesh.

Matt stood at the finish line and watched Jensen line up the horses. Then Jensen came down with his arm. Matt couldn't hear his shout, but he saw the horses leap forward.

Before the race reached the halfway mark it had become a two horse race. The rest were pounding along behind, out front were Dobson's horse and Bolling's old bay, Dynamite. Matt had never seen such a transformation as had taken place in the old horse. Gone was his apathy. He was stretching those long legs, his neck leveled out, the bit tight in his teeth. And he was matching strides with Dobson's horse.

The crowd was yelling wildly. Those with horses in the race had quickly given up hope for their favorites and now were pulling for Billy and his old sway-backed bay. Nobody, it seemed, was cheering for Dobson.

Then a gasp went up behind Matt. Matt saw it, too. Dobson's horse suddenly swerved into the bay. Deliberate, Matt guessed, but there was no way to prove it. But Dynamite was a veteran of the track. An inexperienced horse would have been knocked off stride if not off his feet. But the old bay gave ground to the outside and kept running smoothly.

They thundered on toward town, running hard, but Dobson's horse, Jigger, had broken stride when he swerved into Dynamite. When he regained his stride he was a length behind the bay. And it was a length he never regained.

The cheers were deafening as the bay flashed across the finish line, his heels almost in the face of Dobson's horse. Only when the other horses began slowing down was Billy able to pull the bay to a stop and turn him around. The boy's face was glowing with pride and excitement as he came back and slid to the ground in front of Bolling and Matt.

"We won," Billy exclaimed. "A hundred and fifteen dollars!"

Bolling grinned. "Reckon I ought to thank Dobson for his hundred-dollar donation."

Matt laughed. "Better let well enough alone. I was taught never to tease a skunk when he's mad."

Matt expected Dobson and Gyp to cause trouble now that they had lost the race. But when he looked around for them after turning over the prize money, they had vanished.

CHAPTER IX

Supper was a sullen meal at the Broken S that night. Gyp had spent an hour before supper ranting about the way Dandy Dobson had been cheated out of a hundred dollars in the horse race. Bull had argued with Gyp, for to him it had looked like a clever trick and he admired it even if it had been accomplished by a member of the opposition. His talk would have been entirely different, Jennie thought, if it had been his money that had been lost.

But Gyp had run out of words by the time the meal started. He gulped his food, banging his knife and fork on the plate to emphasize his mood.

"When is Dandy coming out again?" Dolly Sanford asked at the close of the meal.

"In a couple of days," Gyp said. "He's got something to talk over with Jennie."

Gyp scowled at Jennie, then shoved back his chair and stamped out of the house.

"What can he want with me?" Jennie asked, frowning.

"He's well off, Jennie," Bull said in what he considered his persuasive tone of voice. "He'd make a mighty good catch."

Anger soared up in Jennie. "Do you think for a minute I'd marry an outlaw like Dandy Dobson?"

"He's no outlaw," Bull roared. "He's a respectable citizen and a shrewd businessman. He's wealthy now, and he'll be a millionaire before he's done. He knows how to do it, and he'll do it."

"Let him do it," Jennie retorted. "But I don't want any part of it."

Bull scowled at Jennie. "You'd better think it over. You'll never get a better chance to be wealthy."

Bull stamped out of the house, and Jennie turned on Dolly. Dolly was the one who had the good sense in this family.

"Why is he so determined to have me marry Dandy Dobson, Aunt Dolly?" she demanded.

Dolly shrugged. "I don't know. The scheming of men is sometimes beyond me. I know Bull and Gyp have some scheme cooked up with Dandy, but I don't see why they should try to involve you."

Jennie gasped. "You think I'm part of the deal?"

Dolly shrugged again. "I've lived with Bull for a good many years, and that was his bargaining voice tonight. I don't know how they figure to come out on

81

it, but apparently they've promised Dandy you'll be decent to him, at least."

"I'm going to break that promise for them."

Dolly smiled. "Can't say as I blame you, Jennie. I thought once he'd make a good catch for you because he had money. But I've been sleeping on it since. Dandy might have his place but, if I were a young girl, it sure wouldn't be at my table. He's so stuck on himself there ain't room for anybody else to like him. But he considers himself quite a tiger and he'll take some taming."

Jennie kept busy the next few days with work in her garden and around the house. Then the school board offered her the job of painting the interior of the schoolhouse, a job she eagerly accepted.

Then one night, while she got her horse out of the little barn behind the schoolhouse, she heard a horse outside and decided quickly that Curt Henley was stopping by.

Hurriedly she led the horse out of the barn and around to the front of the schoolhouse where the rider had stopped. But she came to a halt at the corner of the building, dismay running through her. It wasn't Curt dismounting in front of the door; it was Dandy Dobson. She thought of ducking back around the building, mounting, and riding home. But he had already seen her.

"I was afraid I'd missed you," he said, leading his horse over to the corner where she was standing. "Gyp said you were here."

"If you had come a little quicker, I might have given you a coat of whitewash. You need it."

He laughed. "Always good for a joke. I like that."

"I'm not in a joking mood, Dandy."

He nodded. "That's just as well. What I want to talk about isn't a joke, either. Are you ready to go home?"

"Just about," Jennie said.

"I'll ride out to the ranch with you," Dandy said. "We can talk as we go."

Suddenly Jennie felt a desire to get it over with. "Let's talk right now. I've got some problems to think out. I want to ride home alone."

Dandy shrugged. "That's fine with me. Has Gyp or Bull said anything about me lately?"

"Nothing that I could believe."

"Do you know how much I own?" he asked, leading his horse up close to Jennie.

"I don't know and I don't care."

Dandy grunted. "You're a queer one if you don't care. You'll change your tune when you find out what I've got to say."

"I doubt it," Jennie said shortly.

"I own the only elevator in Meadows, so I control all the grain in this area. I can name my own price and pay just that. I'm making a big profit on everything I handle. And I've got bigger plans, lots bigger plans."

"Am I supposed to be interested?" Jennie asked.

Color crept up into Dandy's neck, but his voice didn't change. "You will when I tell you what I came for. I want you to marry me, Jennie. I'll make you the happiest woman on earth. You'll have everything you want."

Jennie didn't say anything for a moment.

"Am I supposed to be flattered by your proposal?" she asked after he had waited for an answer so long that anger was reddening his face.

"That's up to you," he said arrogantly. "I don't know of any girl in this country who wouldn't be."

"You're looking at one," Jennie said spiritedly. "I want to make this clear, Mr. Dobson. I wouldn't marry you under any circumstances in the world."

Shock held him speechless for a moment. Then a deep flush swept over his face. "You will," he grated angrily. "Gyp said you would."

"Gyp doesn't run my life."

He stepped forward, clutching her arm. "You've got to marry me. I've got to have you. Besides," he added, seeming to get control of himself again, "you'd be the envy of every woman in the country."

"I'm satisfied the way I am. Now let go my arm."

"You haven't said yet you'd marry me," he said, gripping her arm more tightly.

There was no point in arguing with a man like Dandy Dobson. She'd give him an answer he would understand. She gripped the quirt dangling from her wrist and with a quick stroke brought it down over his neck and back.

With a scream of surprise and pain he fell back from her, and she wheeled and vaulted onto her horse. She had barely turned her mount's head when she heard him scrambling into his saddle.

"I'll get you for that!" he yelled.

Fear gripped her then. She kicked her horse into a full gallop, not heeding the direction he took. Behind her, she heard Dobson's horse coming at a run. And she knew that her pony couldn't outdistance Dobson's race horse for very long.

Her horse had been headed north when she kicked him with her heels, and he didn't change direction. To the north of the school were the mill and the lake, and in a matter of seconds the mill was looming up directly in front of her.

She saw the man standing on the south side of the mill just before he reached up and caught the horse's bridle, pulling him down. Behind, Dobson was coming, but Jennie didn't want to run now. Matt Freeman would give her better protection than she could get by running.

She slid off her horse just as Dobson jerked his horse to a halt and jumped off. A red welt was rising along his neck, and Jennie caught a glimpse of his eyes as he charged forward. Her knees almost gave way and she leaned weakly against the mill. If ever she had looked into a crazy man's eyes, she was doing it then.

"I'll teach you to use a quirt on me," he screamed, and dived for her.

Jennie cringed back against the wall.

Matt's long arm shot out and blocked Dandy's charge.

"This is none of your business, Freeman!" Dandy shouted.

"It's mine now," Matt said, his voice low but the words snapping like breaking bubbles on the surface of a boiling pot. "If you touch her, you've got to go over me to do it."

"That's fine with me." Dandy whipped a fist around that caught Matt on the side of the face and rocked him back against the wall beside Jennie. But Matt used the wall as a catapult to throw himself forward and meet Dandy charging in.

Jennie had seen men fight before, but never had she seen a bloody struggle to match this. Matt was taller and heavier than Dandy, and from the first he had the best of it. But Dandy had lost all reasoning power, and he wouldn't give up. Only when he was beaten into a bloody, almost senseless pulp did he yield.

"Are you satisfied now, Dobson?" Matt asked.

Dandy nodded, spitting blood from cut lips. "For now. But don't think you've heard the last of this, Freeman. I'll get you."

"Any time you feel lucky," Matt said. "I don't know what your trouble with Jennie was, but if I ever hear of you bothering her again, I'm coming after you. And I'll come smoking."

CHAPTER X

Matt Freeman had had several fights in his twenty-five years, but never had he run into such opposition, pound for pound, as he had in Dandy Dobson. Dobson had acted like a crazy man, showing strength that was almost unbelievable in a man his size.

He must have been crazy, Matt decided as he watched him ride up the slope toward town. No man in his right mind would chase a girl the way Dobson had been running after Jennie.

He turned to Jennie, suddenly remembering the fright she had had. She was still leaning against the wall of the mill, but the color was back in her face now.

"Better come inside and rest awhile before you go home," he suggested.

She smiled weakly. "I think I'll accept that invitation. I want to thank you for what you did."

He shook his head. "Don't thank me. It was a pleasure. I already had a score to settle with Dandy Dobson."

"I didn't think you'd ever seen him before the race the other day."

Matt led Jennie inside and found a chair for her. "He paid us a visit one night while we were bringing out the machinery for the mill."

"I hadn't heard about that. Cause trouble?"

"Tried to. All he got out of it was a scar on the back of his hand. You might have seen it."

"I've never noticed it. I can't imagine Dandy laying himself open to the law like that."

"It was night and he was wearing a mask. But there's no question about Dandy being one of the men.

One of the others called him Dandy."

"Who else was on that raid?"

"I couldn't see any faces," Matt said after a second's hesitation.

"Gyp was one, wasn't he?" Jennie asked pointedly.

Matt nodded slowly. "We collected their guns. And one had the initials G. S."

"I'm not surprised. Gyp and Dandy have been very chummy lately. They have some deal cooked up."

Jennie stopped, and Matt waited. The girl was worried about something. Matt found himself wanting to help her.

"I know it's none of my business, Jennie, but Dobson seemed to be pretty riled. Are you having some kind of trouble?"

She looked up, meeting his eyes frankly. "After the fight you just had, you've got a right to know what was behind it. I've never had trouble with Dandy before. He proposed, and of course I turned him down. He seemed to go crazy. Said something about Gyp making a deal."

"Involving you?"

Jennie nodded. "I think so. When he wouldn't let go of my arm, I hit him with my quirt."

Matt grinned. "I'd like to have seen that. He must have thought a lot of you."

"He didn't care a whit about me," Jennie said. "Yet he was determined that I should marry him. I don't know why."

Matt was thoughtful for a minute. This was a new

angle. He could understand why a man might lose his head if the girl he wanted to marry answered him with a quirt lash. But Jennie didn't think Dandy loved her, and Matt wasn't one to question a girl's judgment of such things. If Dandy wanted to marry Jennie for some other reason, it must have something to do with making more money. Dandy Dobson had a reputation for grabbing money at every turn. But what money? And how could marrying Jennie bring it into Dobson's pockets?

"I can see where Gyp and Dobson might make a deal to oust the settlers from this valley," Matt said finally. "Dobson is already doing his part by not paying anything for the grain the farmers raise. But I don't figure Bull and Gyp would go so far as to promise you to Dandy in return for his cooperation."

Jennie nodded. "Bull and Gyp would do that, all right, if they thought it would get rid of the settlers. But that isn't all. Dandy had some other reason for wanting to marry me. I know he did."

"Just getting you would be enough for any man in his right senses," Matt said, then suddenly wheeled toward the stove as he caught Jennie's startled look. "I think you need some strong coffee after that experience."

"It would taste good," she admitted. "Let me make it. Aunt Dolly says I'm a good hand."

She came over to the stove, and he turned to the coffee grinder on the shelf. "I'll have to grind a little. I'll have it ready before the water's hot."

The coffee was good and the conversation right, and before Matt realized it, shadows were creeping into the room. Jennie suddenly got up from her chair.

"I must get home."

Matt rose quickly. "I didn't realize it was so late. I'll ride home with you, if you don't mind. I didn't like the mood Dobson was in when he left."

Jennie nodded. "I'd be glad to have you, Matt. I wouldn't put anything past Dandy now."

It was deep dusk when they left the mill, and as dark as a crescent of a moon would allow it to get before they were halfway to the Broken S. Matt couldn't keep his eyes off the girl beside him, but it wasn't until they reined up within sight of the lights of the Broken S that he realized that something was happening to him.

"I can go on alone now, Matt," Jennie said. "There might be trouble if you came in."

He dismounted. "You're probably right. I've had enough trouble for one day. But I'll stay here and see that you get to the house all right."

"I want to thank you for everything, Matt," Jennie said, stretching down her hand.

He took her hand and looked up into her face, outlined by the dark sky and early evening stars. The feeling that had been growing on him since they left the mill reached a climax and he moved involuntarily, giving her hand a little tug.

She slid from her saddle, landing lightly in front of him. She seemed to sense what he was going to do, for she whispered, "You shouldn't, Matt."

But she had no chance to say any more before he kissed her. For a moment she returned his kiss and the world reduced itself for Matt to the girl he held in his arms.

Then just as suddenly as it had happened she pushed away from him and the spell was broken.

"We mustn't," she said, her voice barely above a whisper. "I guess I was too upset to think."

Matt knew what she meant.

"Henley?" he said, his voice lifeless.

She nodded. "I was carried away by gratitude, I guess. I am grateful to you, Matt, very grateful. But—"

"Sure," he broke in. "I understand. It was my fault; I'm sorry. Now you'd better get down to the house."

She hesitated a moment, then mounted swiftly and drove her horse recklessly down the slope to the barn a short distance from the house.

Matt waited until he saw her in the light of the open door as she went into the house; then he mounted his horse and turned him back toward town. But his thoughts stayed there on the knoll overlooking the Broken S. He had come to his senses and realized how far out of bounds he had stepped. But it didn't change his feeling a bit. He was in love with Jennie Kent. He knew she was Curt Henley's girl and probably very soon would be his wife. But that didn't change anything for Matt. He wished it could.

The gentlemanly thing to do, of course, would have

been to step back to the sidelines and say it didn't matter. He might step back, but he couldn't be a hypocrite and say it didn't matter. It did matter. And after tonight, it would always matter.

Matt abandoned his idea of laying aside his guns. After his trouble with Gyp Sanford and now with Dandy Dobson, he knew he had to have them. He took to wearing them all the time he wasn't eating or sleeping. And he used three boxes of cartridges from Falley's hardware and began to practice with them.

He discovered the first day of practice that he hadn't lost his touch. The guns came out of the holsters smoothly and his aim was good. His speed was not quite as great as of old, but practice soon corrected that.

With the help of Billy and John, he set up some targets along the shore of the lake upstream from the mill. Each day he spent a little time at those targets.

He was there one afternoon when Sid Bolling came down the slope from town, his bowed legs holding his feet so far apart that as he walked his body rocked like a boat on a rough sea. Matt holstered his gun and waited for him.

"Howdy, Sid," Matt greeted him. "What's wrong?"

Bolling was puffing from his exertion. "What makes you think anything is wrong?"

"You wouldn't be walking all the way down here if there wasn't."

"I sure wouldn't if I could straddle a horse without it half killing me. But something is wrong, all right. Dandy Dobson is in town and he's getting likkered up.

He's in Baxter's Drug Store bragging about what he's going to do to you."

"Like meeting me with guns?"

Bolling nodded. "Yeah. You can take care of yourself all right, can't you? I don't know how fast he is."

"I doubt if he's the fastest man I've ever seen. Does anyone know why he's after me?"

Bolling dropped down on the grass at the edge of the water. "I reckon everybody knows it. Billy came into town the other night right after you had your fight with Dandy and bragged about the way you whipped him."

"Nothing to brag about, whipping a little banty like him. How much did Billy tell?"

"Plenty. Enough so that everybody's pulling for you. He told how Dandy was chasing Jennie. That was enough in itself. Then he described the fight and how Dandy threatened you afterward, and you told him to keep away from Jennie or you'd come after him and you'd come smoking."

Matt was thoughtful for a moment. "Looks like I've got a fight on my hands and no way out of it."

"I've got my doubts," Bolling said. "I figure Dandy is cut from pretty thin cloth and, when it comes right down to it, he'll back down."

"I hope so," Matt said. "I don't want to have to kill him." Bolling suddenly lowered his voice. "More company," he said. Matt turned to look toward the mill. Preston Jok was striding rapidly toward them.

"Looks like my trip was wasted," Jok said as he

reached Matt. "I suppose Sid has told you Dobson is in town looking for you?"

Matt nodded. "But he thinks maybe Dandy is too weak-kneed to force the issue."

Jok turned to glance back toward town. "That's very possible. But as long as he's alive he's apt to shoot you in the back."

"Not much I can do about that."

"There's plenty you can do," Jok said quickly. "Dobson has already bragged about how he's going to gun you down. Nobody could blame you for forcing the issue now. You'd be in the clear and you wouldn't be in danger of an ambush."

"Maybe I can't beat Dandy."

Jok nodded toward the targets. "From what I hear, you know how to handle a gun. I doubt if Dobson is so fast."

"Do you always carry two guns?" Bolling asked, indicating the twin gun belts Matt was wearing.

"Habit, I guess," Matt said, shrugging. "I never use but one at a time. But I've been in spots where an extra loaded gun came in mighty handy."

"Wrong side of the law?" Jok suggested.

"The law wasn't involved," Matt said. "It was a range war."

"Are you going after Dobson now?" Jok asked.

"No," Matt said. "If he wants me he knows where he can find me. We're grinding this afternoon."

"Using up your old wheat?" Bolling asked. "Who's buying the flour?"

94

"Some of the merchants at Meadows. They've had a lot of demands for this flour made with the rollers. I'm going to grind what wheat I've got and have the bins ready for the new wheat this fall."

Billy came running from the mill, and Matt hurried to meet him. "We're out of sacks," Billy yelled. "Shall I shut down?"

"There are more in the empty grain bin on the right," Matt said, breaking into a run. "If we hurry, the flour bin will hold the flour till we get the sacks and we won't have to shut down."

They had almost enough flour to make a load by quitting time that night, and Matt looked at the pile of fifty-pound sacks in satisfaction.

"We'll load up in the morning and take the flour over to Meadows. This will make a good start."

"It's the finish that counts," John said gloomily. "I don't like this Dandy Dobson business."

Matt shrugged. "I don't, either. But there's nothing I can do about it." He was too tired to think about Dobson tonight.

Before starting to load the wagon the next morning, Matt reached for his gun belts. It was then he discovered he had only one gun for his two holsters. He looked over the room, bewildered at the loss. A gun was something a man didn't just leave lying around. Finally he decided he must have left it out at the target area the afternoon before when Billy had come running to him asking about sacks for the flour. He had taken off the belts in such a hurry when he first came in yesterday afternoon that he hadn't noticed the loss.

He jammed the one gun into his holster and started for the door. Then he stopped. Something about the way that gun had sounded when it slid into the holster caught his ear. He lifted the gun out again and tipped the holster, looking into it.

A bit of paper caught his eye. It was stuffed in the very bottom, where ordinarily the muzzle of the gun wouldn't rustle it. But this morning the gun muzzle had caught the paper.

He fished the paper out and read the note on it. Excitement poured through him as he read. He recognized Fred's writing immediately.

"Matt," it read: "These guns should be given to you in case anything happens to me. I'm fighting Gyp Sanford in a few minutes. There's a steel box under a loose board in the back of the mill close to the waterwheel. See that it is taken care of. Fred."

Matt stared at the note a moment, then stuffed it in his pocket. He forgot about his other gun as he turned into the mill. It wasn't very light in the back of the mill, for there were only two windows. From one of the windows he could look out on the waterwheel, motionless now, and the creek as it meandered down past town.

Quickly Matt began searching for a loose board and found it close to the window. The end of the board lifted easily for a few inches. He struck a match and peered underneath. A small steel box was nestled between the joists. He lifted the box out on the floor.

Fishing with nervous fingers through his pockets, he located the key and fitted it into the lock. He took the papers to the window and began to leaf through them.

They had nothing to do with either him or Fred. They seemed to be the personal papers of Molly Kent. He shuffled through them, finally stopping at one that caught his eye. The last will of Molly Kent.

He scanned it. It was brief, using the first half of the single page to declare void any previously made will. Then it willed everything to Molly's daughter, Jennie Kent. Matt's eyes widened as he read what that amounted to. The Lazy K, one half section deeded land with buildings and the cattle under the Lazy K brand that ranged the three thousand acres of open range that had been used by the Lazy K for years. Also nearly fifty thousand dollars in cash and bonds to be transferred to Jennie upon probation of the will.

Matt put the papers back in the box and squatted on his heels, staring at them. Jennie apparently had no idea she was a rich young woman. Then he thought of the man, Sim Carlton, who had been killed trying to keep the key to this box from falling into the wrong hands. Now it was Matt's responsibility. Should he take it to Jennie?

Quickly he decided against that. If whoever wanted that box and the will found out Jennie had it, her life would be in danger. Men had been killed for far less than the money represented by that will. In fact, Carlton had been killed merely for keeping the key to this box. No one knew Matt had the key or that he had found the box. It was best that he keep it that way until he figured out what he should do with it.

He locked the box and put it back between the floor joists. But his mind clung to that will. He could take it to Jok. Jok was a lawyer. He could probate the will and turn over Jennie's inheritance to her. Suddenly it struck Matt that Dobson might know about this will and be trying to marry Jennie's fortune.

He thought about Jennie then and how this would affect her. It would mean she and Curt Henley could get married immediately and go back east where he would have money enough to set himself up in a fine practice. As for Matt's feelings about Jennie, they wouldn't change. But they would have to be buried beyond recovery now. He might otherwise have decided to contest Henley's claim to Jennie's affections. But not now. Jennie would be a wealthy lady. And a wealthy lady should be married to a professional man, not a miller.

A shout from the front of the building snapped Matt out of his gloomy mood. He recognized Billy's voice and heard running feet as John went to meet him. He hurried out to the front of the building in time to see Billy throw himself off his horse and run up to the door where John was waiting.

"Dandy Dobson was killed last night," Billy panted. "Murdered."

"Murdered?" John exclaimed. "Who did it?"

"Nobody knows. One man said it was you, Matt. I called him a liar."

"Thanks, Billy," Matt said, his mind in a turmoil. "This may not mean anything to me and it may mean a lot. What's the general sentiment in town?"

Billy frowned. "A lot of people knew Dandy was out to get you, and some of them figure you beat him to it."

"How do they know it was murder?"

"He was shot in the back."

"Might be smart for you to hightail it out of here till things cool off," John suggested.

"Then everybody would be sure I was guilty," Matt said. "All I can do is wait and see what happens. Where was Dobson killed?"

"Up here on the lake shore," Billy said, pointing.

Matt frowned. "How come John and I didn't hear the shot?"

Billy shook his head. "All I know is that's what they said."

"Well, let's load the flour," Matt said. "We've got to deliver that today."

But the load wasn't yet ready to roll when the marshal, Pete Guckert, and a half-dozen men from the town came down the slope toward the mill.

"You should have lit out," John said softly as they watched the men approach.

"They've got no proof against me," Matt said.

Guckert came forward, his self-importance pushing his chest out behind the star. He glanced around at the men behind him, then came up to within a few feet of the three waiting by the wagon.

99

"You're under arrest, Freeman," he said dramatically.

"For what?" Matt demanded.

"Murdering Dandy Dobson."

"Prove it," Matt challenged.

"We'll do that in the courtroom," Guckert said smugly as if he felt his statement were a gem of brilliance.

"What evidence do you have? Hearsay?"

"We've got your gun. It fired the shot that killed Dobson. Then you threw it in the edge of the lake."

A chill ran over Matt. "Where's the gun?"

"I've got it," Guckert said importantly, pulling it from the waist of his pants. "Ain't this yours?"

Matt looked at it, and his heart sank. It was his gun, all right.

CHAPTER XI

Matt had been in the marshal's office before, but this was the first time he had been in the single cell jail at the back. The men with Guckert at the mill had all gone back to other business as soon as the marshal had locked the door behind Matt. Guckert flopped down in his chair and propped his feet up on the little scarred desk.

He seemed to feel unusually talkative. Matt wondered if it wasn't reaction to fear. For he had the marshal tagged as a man who didn't have too much stiffness in his backbone.

"Just how long do you figure you can keep me here?" Matt demanded.

"Till you have your trial and are hanged legally."

"You don't think you can make that story go over about me shooting a man, then leaving the gun right there to condemn me, do you?"

"You didn't leave it on purpose," Guckert said confidently. "I interrupted you."

"You did?" Matt exclaimed in surprise.

"Sure. Dobson was bragging about gunning you down, and when he left the drug store last night and headed down toward the mill I followed. I figured I'd better protect you. But he went on somewhere, and I hung around the mill so nothing would happen to you."

"That was thoughtful of you," Matt said sarcastically.

"I didn't know you was a killer then. Anyway, I heard a shot a few minutes later up by the lake, and I ran up there. I heard somebody run away, and I found Dobson shot in the back. We went back early this morning and found your gun at the edge of the water. Same kind of gun that fired the shot that killed Dobson, and there's just one empty shell in it."

Matt sat on the one little stool that the cell boasted and thought it over. This was a lot more serious than he had anticipated. Every bit of evidence pointed to him. Even the motive was well established. If it had been an open gun fight, he'd have had the community with him. But shooting a man in the back was some-

thing else. Only a few close friends who were convinced he was innocent would stick by him now.

The day ran along. Guckert went out and stayed
away till afternoon. Matt lay down on the hard cot and
dozed. Voices out front roused him. He didn't move,
and the voices droned on. What they said didn't
interest him, but one voice snapped his mind alert. He
had heard that voice somewhere before. Somewhere
where he hadn't seen the man's face. Still he didn't
move. If he looked at the speaker, the spell would be
gone. And he had to remember where he had heard
that voice.

Then it struck him. The second night he had been
here, down at the mill, when he had come home after
talking to Larabee and Jensen. The man had
demanded the box then. So here was one of the men
who was trying to rob Jennie Kent of her inheritance.

He spun his legs off the cot and looked out through
the bars. There was a man talking in a low voice to
Pete Guckert. But it was Guckert's voice Matt had
recognized. He had seen him several times since that
night at the mill, but he hadn't recognized the voice
until he heard it without seeing the face.

But Guckert wasn't the big boss. That night at the
mill Matt had decided that the man prodding the gun
in his back was not the one who gave the orders. And
now that he knew it *had* been Guckert at the mill, he
was certain of it. Guckert was neither smart enough
nor courageous enough to be the power behind the
scheme to strip Jennie of her inheritance.

There was a little activity in front of the marshal's office during the afternoon. Matt didn't know whether that was unusual or not. But the men coming into town during the late afternoon were unusual, he knew.

"Who are all the people in town?" Matt asked when Guckert brought him his supper.

"Mostly people from Meadows," the marshal said. "They're talking a little nasty."

Matt knew what that meant. Dobson had been a business man in Meadows and, regardless of what kind of man he was, he had some friends there. With the right kind of talk, a mob could be whipped up easily. There would be a lot of impressionable hombres right here in Tumbleweed who might go along with the movement.

Maybe it had been planned this way, Matt thought. Lots of people disliked Dobson, but he didn't know of anyone who hated him enough to kill him. Maybe the ultimate goal was to get rid of Matt. Dobson's quarrel with Matt had set the stage. If Matt had been ambushed, public sentiment would have run down the killer. But by accusing Matt of murder and getting a mob to hang him before a legal trial could show up the flaws in the evidence, the schemer could dispose of Matt without danger to himself.

The sun burned its path down the western side of the sky and into the prairie, taking the daylight with it as it disappeared. In the gloom of his cell, Matt waited, looking out through the bars of his one window. Across the street and half a block down, lights burned in the drug store, and there was no misinterpreting the tone of the voices coming from there.

"Think I'll go out and see what's going on," Guckert said, and stalked through the front door.

Matt watched him go, thinking that he'd be of little help if a mob did storm the jail. A mob was in the making, and he wondered who was pushing it. He couldn't imagine anyone here in Tumbleweed being excited enough over Dobson's death to stir up a mob to lynch the man accused of his murder. The driving force came from Meadows or perhaps from someone here who had a motive other than avenging Dobson's death. Matt preferred to believe the latter.

A hiss at his cell window took him back there. He peered out, bobbing his head from one side to the other, but he couldn't see anyone. Whoever wanted to attract his attention was being careful not to be seen by anyone outside, or perhaps he didn't want Matt to see him.

"Are you in there, Freeman?" came a whisper.

"Haven't found a way to get out yet," Matt said.

"I can get you out," the voice said. "All I ask is some cooperation."

"Meaning what?" Matt asked. He tried to place the voice, but the only thing he could be sure of was that it was a man's whisper. It might be Guckert, but Matt doubted that. This voice had more life in it than Guckert's lazy drawl.

"You give me that box you've got hidden when I get you out. Agree?"

Matt hesitated only a second. "No," he said. Turning over that box would be the same as turning over Jennie's inheritance. Just how someone else could get that inheritance by destroying Molly Kent's will was something Matt didn't understand. But he could think of no other reason anyone would go to such lengths to get that box.

"Then stay there till they come and hang you," the voice muttered.

Matt heard the footsteps retreat, and again the only sound coming into the cell was the rumble down at the drug store. Guckert came in after a few minutes and propped himself in his chair close to the door.

"Talking pretty nasty," he said. "Looks like we're got a big night ahead."

Matt ignored him. Guckert was now in the enemy camp so far as Matt was concerned. After the visit a few minutes ago from the man demanding the box, he was convinced that the box held the key to his being where he was now. His arrest had been intended as a pry to get the box from him. Now that that hadn't worked, he wondered how far this would go. Maybe even to hanging him so they could tear the mill apart board by board till they found it. He wouldn't be the first man to be killed for possession of that box.

Guckert dozed in his chair, and Matt stood by the window listening and watching. A shadow flitted across his vision, and he saw John inching up toward the window. Matt held up a finger to caution John to silence.

"We've got to get you out of there," John whispered when he reached the bars. "That mob means business."

Matt nodded. "Any ideas?"

"Billy's at the mill. I think we can force Guckert to turn you loose if we get here before that mob gets moving."

"I'll need a good horse," Matt said. Running away wasn't going to help him clear himself. But now he was sure that staying here meant hanging.

"We'll find one," John said. "Something else happened today. Just at dark tonight we caught somebody planting dynamite under the floor of our wagon load of flour. We chased him off but couldn't see who it was."

"Didn't want that flour delivered," Matt said, but his mind had suddenly gone off on a tangent. He whipped a glance at the marshal, who was still dozing in his chair. "Listen, John, I've got an idea that beats a horse."

"Nothing beats a horse when you're in a hurry," John said.

"This will," Matt insisted. "Unload most of the flour from that wagon and leave the dynamite there. Hitch up the team and bring the wagon up behind Sid's livery barn. Then get me out of here and I'll take the wagon. They'll never expect me to make a get-away in a wagon."

"But the dynamite will be dangerous," John objected.

"It won't explode just from shaking. But if they chase me, I can stage a big explosion. It's better than taking a chance on a horse."

Slowly John nodded. "Might be at that. We'll do it. But we'll have to hurry."

John slid away into the darkness, and Matt looked again at the dozing marshal. It wouldn't be hard for John and Billy to spring him if they got here before the mob. For Matt didn't doubt for an instant now that the mob was going to come. The effort to scare him into parting with the box had been made and had failed, but the murmur of the mob hadn't slackened. In fact, it had almost doubled. Which meant that the embers were being stirred into flame.

The minutes dragged. The murmur from down the street was punctuated now and then by a shout. The breaking point was nearing. He strained his ears to catch the squeak of iron on sand that would tell him the wagon was being brought up to the livery barn. But he heard nothing. Probably John and Billy hadn't had time yet to get things ready.

He tried to sit on his cot but he couldn't. He had to keep moving. Any minute now something would break. It had to. If only he could do something! But all he could do was wait and hope.

Guckert opened one eye and squinted in his direction. "Getting nervous?" he asked carelessly.

Matt didn't answer him. He kept pacing his cell. He estimated the time John had been gone and listened to the sounds down the street. It wouldn't be long now.

Then it came. Matt felt as if a leaden weight had dropped in his stomach, and despair which was almost a sickness swept over him. John and Billy were too late.

The drug store was spewing out men, a dozen or more. And when they turned toward the marshal's office, there was no mistaking their intent. Whoever had primed them for this job had done it well.

Matt glanced at Guckert. He was awake now, and he reached for a rifle leaning against the wall. But he showed little enthusiasm for his job, and Matt knew the mob would get little opposition from him.

The mob hit the front door of the marshal's office, and a man yelled, "Give us that prisoner, Guckert."

"Get away," Guckert shouted. "He's going to get a trial."

Matt felt as if he were watching a scene from a rehearsed play, each actor repeating the lines he had learned.

"You can't hold him, Guckert," the man outside shouted. "We're coming in after him."

The door burst open, and Matt realized Guckert hadn't even had it locked. Matt didn't know any of the men who charged across the room, snatched the keys from Guckert's desk and opened his cell door. He had expected to see Gyp Sanford, at least, but there wasn't a man from Tumbleweed.

"You're out of your territory, aren't you?" Matt said, his voice tight and dry.

"You killed Dandy Dobson," the leader roared.

"You're going to pay for it. He was our friend."

Matt thought of saying more but decided against it. There wasn't anything, not even time, to be gained by arguing with these men. Matt guessed they were being well paid for their work, and words weren't going to slow them or swerve them from their goal. Guckert was standing back against the wall as the men led Matt outside.

"Good job of upholding the law," Matt threw sarcastically at the marshal.

"He's got good sense," one of the mob said. "No point in getting hurt just to protect a murderer."

"Where will we string him up?" one man asked, looking up and down the street. "No trees here big enough."

"How about the livery barn?" the leader said, pointing. "Hang him to the ridge pole out front."

"Let's go. Somebody get a horse."

A rope was brought, and Matt's hands were tied behind his back. Then he was mounted on a horse one of the men got from the hitchrack in front of the drug store.

There had been a light in the office in the front of the livery barn, but Matt noticed now that it was gone. Maybe Sid Bolling had just gone to bed, or maybe he didn't want to get involved.

The horse was led down the street to the front of the livery barn. There it was stopped directly under the long beam which extended out six or eight feet from the barn roof. One man tossed the end of a long rope over the ridge pole just as the big doors in the center of the barn were thrown open. Sid Bolling stood there, a heavy scowl on his face.

"Get out of here!" he shouted. "You don't use my barn for a necktie party."

"Aw, shut up," one man snarled, and gave Bolling a push, sending him sprawling back into the barn.

"If you don't want to leave him dangling here till morning, you can cut him down after we leave," another man said.

Bolling disappeared, and Matt felt the noose slip over his head.

"Better blindfold him," one man said. "There's nothing left in this world for him to see."

A neckerchief was brought out, and a man stepped up to tie it over Matt's eyes. But just then Matt heard a yell from the back of the barn and jerked his head away from the blindfold to look through the open door of the barn. It was dark inside, but a pale light from the other wall told him the back door of the barn was open, too.

Then came the thunder of pounding hoofs. In a flash Matt realized what was happening. Bolling's horses in the corral behind the barn were being driven pell mell through the open doors. The men around Matt, intent on the hanging, were slower to realize what was taking place; they stood in amazement as the first horse, the sway-backed bay that had won the race, charged into the street.

Matt jabbed his heels into his mount and crowded

him out of line of the stampeding horses, then threw himself out of the saddle and let the horse run with the rest. Not all the men in the mob were so lucky. All were afoot, and it was a veritable avalanche of horse-flesh that crowded through the doors into the street.

The second the mass of horses was past, Matt dodged into the barn. The noose was still trailing from his neck and his hands were bound, but there was too much confusion outside for anyone to notice him. Two of the mob had been trampled by the horses.

A hand reached out and jerked the noose off Matt's neck. "I've got my knife," Bolling whispered. "I can cut those ropes quicker than I can untie them."

While Bolling sawed on the ropes, he whispered more instructions. "John brought your wagon, and it's sitting outside ready to go. Better move fast. These jaspers will come to their senses pretty soon and get horses."

"I'll be a long way from here by then. Thanks, Sid."

With his hands free, Matt ran out the back door and vaulted over the corral fence. The wagon was there, the horses tugging at the lines. John shoved the reins into Matt's hand as he reached the seat.

"They're ready to run," John said. "That stampede Sid started got them excited."

"Thanks, John," Matt said. "Don't be surprised at anything that happens to this wagon."

John jumped off the wagon, and Matt slackened the lines. The team hit the collars with a lunge, and Matt guided them into the road leading toward Meadows.

The jangle of the harness and grind of the wheels made more noise than Matt liked, but speed was more important now than stealth. With as much confusion as there was back there, his flight might not even be noticed.

A mile from town, Matt pulled the team to a stop and listened. The night was quiet, the stillness broken only by a dog owl over in the prairie dog town to the south. Pursuit hadn't started yet. Maybe it wouldn't start at all. Those men had nothing at stake except the money they were being paid for their work. And since some of them had been hurt by the stampeding horses, they might have lost their enthusiasm for the job.

Matt started the team on at a slower pace. He had to consider his next move now. Legally he was a wanted man. The evidence was strong against him. And running away wouldn't help his cause any.

Besides, he couldn't just keep running till he was out of the country, which was what instinct told him to do. He had more than just his own reputation at stake. There was that box hidden under the floor in the back of the mill. He suddenly remembered the note Fred had left him. Had he lost it where someone might find it? He reached into his pocket, and relief swept over him when his fingers touched it. Carefully he tore it to shreds and threw it into the road.

But the box was still at the mill. And whoever was so intent on getting him out of the way would now try to find it. Jennie would never get her rightful inheritance if that will wasn't turned over to the right people. And it was Matt's job to do that.

But first he would have to prove his innocence in Dobson's murder. If he didn't, he would be subject to arrest the minute he showed his face back in Tumbleweed.

It left him but one choice, and it was a precarious one. He had to stay close to the scene and yet he must keep hidden from the law. He thought of the dynamite lashed to the bottom of the wagon box. An explosion, if it was powerful enough, would leave little trace of what had existed before it went off.

Matt mulled the idea over, working out details in his mind as the horses covered the ground to the east. Finally he pulled the horses down and listened carefully for a full minute. There was no sound of pursuit. He nodded in satisfaction. He would need time for this.

Wrapping the lines around the brake lever, he climbed down and got under the wagon. He whistled softly as he saw the stick of dynamite fastened to each bolster. Enough to blow five wagons sky high. Well, that suited his plan fine.

He drove the wagon over next to a steep chalk bluff and stopped, unhitching the horses. He turned one horse loose, giving it a slap, and tied the other to a wheel. Then he took a singletree, stuck it between two spokes of a wheel and finally managed to break it. Just in case there was enough of the wagon left to tell some of the story, he wanted it to look as if there had been a runaway.

He broke pieces of leather off the harness and tossed them on the front of the wagon. Then he tore off the tail of his shirt and the cuff of his pants and threw the pieces up in the seat. Regretfully he took off his boots and put them in the wagon. Pieces of them were certain to be found. With flour and wood splattered over this whole area, it was going to be hard to say that Matt hadn't been right in the center of the explosion, too.

Then, when everything was in readiness, Matt stooped down and struck a match, touching it to the fuse of the nearest stick of dynamite. The others would go when the blast from the first hit them.

Seeing the fuse begin to sputter, Matt wheeled and threw himself on the horse, kicking him in the sides. The horse had run himself about out, and his response to Matt's urging was slow.

Matt brought the end of the line down over the horse's hips. He had to get some distance from that wagon before it exploded or he might as well have stayed right on the seat.

The horse leaped forward at the unaccustomed lashing, but his foot hit a rock that had fallen from the bluff, and he stumbled and fell. As Matt sailed over his head, he realized he wasn't out of range of that blast.

And the next instant the whole world seemed to explode.

CHAPTER XII

Jennie heard about Dobson's murder with mixed feelings. Although she was sorry he had been killed, she couldn't find it in her heart to say she was sorry he was no longer around to annoy her. But she was most dismayed by the report that Matt Freeman had been arrested for Dobson's murder.

She was certain he was innocent. He might have killed Dobson in a fair fight, but never with a shot in the back. His fight with Dobson the day Dandy had proposed to her was probably the basis for his arrest now. So maybe she was partly to blame for Matt's trouble.

She couldn't get it off her mind. At noon both Bull and Gyp were swearing vengeance against Matt. Dandy had been a friend of the Broken S, Gyp and Bull declared.

Jennie rode into town during the afternoon with a vague idea of talking to Matt in jail. Maybe she could do something for him. But Guckert wouldn't let her in to see Matt.

In a way, she decided, it was probably best. More than likely there wasn't anything she could do. And her last meeting with Matt was still too fresh in her mind. She didn't want to remember that. But she couldn't forget it, try as she would. She wondered sometimes if she would ever forget it. Matt had taken all the blame himself for what had happened, but she knew he hadn't been entirely to blame.

She had practically invited him to kiss her, and when he had, she had turned away, letting him blame himself for his impulses.

She didn't stop to see Curt today. Her mind was too full of other things, and she didn't want to break into his office hours. She intended to let her man do his work without undue interruption from her. She might as well get used to it now.

But she lay awake that night, finding it hard to clear her mind for sleep.

Sometime before she went to sleep, Jennie heard a rumble like thunder. It had come from the east and it took her to the window. There were no clouds, and thunderstorms nearly always came up from the northwest here. She stood at the window for a while, looking out on the still night, wondering about the rumble. Then, when the night remained silent, she went back to bed and eventually to sleep.

She rode into town the next morning, but she made a detour by Jensen's homestead. There, in a little flower garden, was Suzy on her knees, pulling weeds.

"Good morning, Suzy," Jennie said.

Suzy smiled. "Good morning, Jennie. What do you think of my flowers?"

"Nice," Jennie said, nodding.

But she was thinking to herself that the girl was even prettier than the flowers, and she could not blame Curt for being attracted to her.

Coming into town, she rode by the mill. The door was closed and it was deathly quiet. A shiver ran over her, she couldn't tell why. Matt was just being held in jail. Being in jail and being convicted of a crime were two different things. Somehow Matt would be proved innocent of Dobson's murder.

She rode on into town, passing the minister, Mark Tuttle, working in the church yard. He lifted a hand and spoke, but there was none of the usual cheerfulness in his voice. A puzzled frown began to furrow Jennie's forehead. There was an atmosphere here in town this morning that she didn't like.

She nudged her horse into a trot. She wanted to get to Curt's office. She could get rid of this mood there. The street seemed deserted except for Sid Bolling, sitting with his chair propped back against the front of the livery stable.

There were no patients in the doctor's office, but one look at Curt's face told Jennie she wasn't going to be cheered here this morning.

"What's the matter with everybody, Curt?" she asked, crossing to his desk.

He pulled up a chair for her. "Guess we're all feeling down in the dumps," Henley said. "Most of us liked Matt Freeman pretty well."

A chill ran over Jennie, and her tongue seemed thick and half paralyzed when she tried to talk. "What's the matter with Matt? Isn't he in jail?"

"He was," Henley said, dropping back in his chair behind the desk. "But last night some hoodlums from Meadows worked up a mob and took him out to hang him."

117

Jennie gasped. "Hang him?"

"They didn't get the job done," Henley said quickly. "They had the rope around his neck and were set to hang him from the ridge pole of Bolling's barn. But Sid ran some loose horses through and Matt got away. Two of the fellows were hurt pretty bad by the horses. I had to fix them up."

"Then Matt escaped?" Jennie said, relief in her voice.

"Right then. He drove a wagon toward Meadows. Somebody had planted several sticks of dynamite in the wagon. From what we can make out, Matt must have had a runaway and the team broke loose. The wagon crashed into the bluff and exploded."

Jennie nodded numbly. "And Matt?"

"We found pieces of his boots and bits of clothing. He must have been right in the middle of it. There was such a shambles, it's hard to tell."

"Couldn't he still be alive?"

"Only by a miracle. There must have been enough dynamite on that wagon to blow up a freight train."

Jennie was silent. Matt Freeman dead! It didn't seem possible. She tried to get it out of her mind. Why should that paralyze her thinking? Had Matt Freeman meant so much to her? The thought shocked her, so she changed the topic.

"I've been thinking, Curt, about your practice back east. Are you still in a hurry to get back there?"

"I guess so," Henley said. "I was reared in the east, and that's where I belong. I don't like jobs like I had last night, patching up men who have been trampled by horses. And there'll be gunshot wounds to treat here, too. As soon as I make enough to set up a good practice, I want to go east."

"Will it take long?"

"Not too long, I hope." Henley leaned close to Jennie. "But you were the one who wanted me to come here. Why the change?"

"I just wanted to know if you'd changed."

He got up and came around the desk. "I haven't, Jennie. And I haven't changed in my thinking about you. As soon as I can, I want to go back east with you as my wife."

Jennie stood up. "I just wanted to hear you say it, Curt. A girl likes to have things put into words once in a while so she knows they haven't changed."

Henley smiled. "They haven't. I'm afraid I've neglected you lately, Jennie. I'll hurry through my work and be out to see you more."

"That's all right, Curt. Tend to your business first. It's more important now."

Jennie rode back to the Broken S, her mind far from easy. She had Curt's assurance that there had been no change in their status. But he hadn't shown the enthusiasm for going back east that he had had before. Nor had his promise to take her back as his wife held the usual eagerness. Curt was changing. Maybe even he didn't realize it yet. But she knew. She could feel it. And she wondered if she were changing, too.

Instantly her mind whipped back to Matt Freeman,

and a wave of despair washed over her. Matt was dead. There was nothing she could do about that. But if he were alive, would she find her loyalty to Curt Henley slipping? No, she told herself. Curt was her man. He had come out here just because she had wanted him to. She wouldn't let him down now, no matter what happened.

The afternoon slipped by.

Just before supper a rider came into the yard, and Jennie hurried to the window. She frowned a little when she saw the lawyer, Preston Jok. She had never known him to come to the Broken S before, and she wondered what his business here could be.

Bull and Gyp were down by the barn. Jennie could see by their cautious approach as they came up to the visitor that they were wondering about his mission, too.

Jennie picked up the empty water pail and went out to the well to get water, taking her time, her ear turned to the talk out by the hitchrack.

"I've taken over the mill in town," she heard Jok say. "I loaned Freeman the money to buy the rollers so, with him dead, I took over on the mortgage he gave me."

"What's that supposed to mean to us?" Bull demanded sourly.

Jennie started cranking the windlass slowly, bringing up a pail of water. She wished the windlass wouldn't squeak so. It interfered with her hearing.

"I'm closing the mill," she heard Jok say before the

squeaking windlass drowned out his words.

The bucket came to the surface, and Jennie poured the water into her pail, then dropped the bucket back into the well. She turned toward the house with the water, and again she could hear talk in the yard.

"So there's no reason for any trouble between us," Jok said.

"I reckon you're better at talking than you are at fighting," Gyp said distrustfully.

Jok laughed and reined out of the yard. Jennie took her water pail inside. She wondered about Jok's visit. Was he trying to make a deal to keep peace? Everyone knew Jok had located the settlers on the best land in the valley and had stood by them in all their troubles. Maybe he had bought peace from the Broken S by closing the mill, at least temporarily, and now there would be no more trouble. Jennie hoped so.

Gyp's mood was dark and venomous when the men came in to supper. He growled about the food and finally turned on Jennie as she brought in a platter of eggs.

"Are you still stuck on that doctor of yours?"

"Yes, if it's any of your business," Jennie said testily.

"I'm going to make that mealy-mouthed pill thrower some of my business. I was over to see Suzy this afternoon, and there he was fussing over her like a sick calf. If I catch him out there one more time, he's going to have to look at me through smoke. Nobody steals my girl without a fight."

Jennie turned back to the kitchen. There was no point in arguing with Gyp. The more anyone talked to him, the wilder he became. She must see Curt soon and make him promise never to visit Suzy except when he was sure Gyp wasn't around. Gyp was a braggart, but he wasn't making idle boasts now. He would demand a gunsmoke showdown with Curt if he became convinced Curt was making a play for Suzy.

Jennie stared out the window. Curt was no fighter. There could be only one outcome to such a fight. There was a void deep inside her now, left by that dynamite blast last night. What would there be if Curt too were killed?

CHAPTER XIII

It was a deathly silent world on which Matt opened his eyes. The stars were bright but the land was dark. He sat up gingerly. There was a blur before his eyes left by the brilliant flash of light which was the last thing he remembered seeing. It couldn't have been more than a minute or so ago.

He sat still for a time, letting his aching body get used to taking orders from his brain again. The horse he had fallen behind when the blast shook him loose from his senses was lying in front of him, but it was dead, though its flesh was still quivering. Except for the protection of that bulky body, Matt would have been dead, too.

Every inch of him seemed to be bruised or

scratched. There was a sliver driven deep into the flesh of his left shoulder.

But the thing that made the night seem eerie was the total lack of sound. Many times he had thought that things around him were quiet. But he realized now that he had never known absolute silence before. There wasn't the hum of an insect, the chirp of a cricket, or the faint whisper of the night wind moving through the grass. There was nothing. He had been shut out of the world. He fought down the panic that started to grip him.

Getting shakily to his feet, he stood for a moment getting his bearings. Relief swept over him as he realized there were no bones broken. Gingerly he started moving toward the creek, which he knew couldn't be more than a hundred yards to the north.

It was slow going, with his aching and bruised muscles protesting every step. And he was in his sock feet. There was no point in looking for his boots. They'd be scattered over ten acres now. Anyway, he had put them there to be found by those investigating. He wanted them to think he had been blown to bits. If they thought he was dead, the law's search for him would be called off and somebody might make a move he wouldn't make otherwise.

At the creek, he knelt and rammed his head into the water. Tumbleweed Creek was spring-fed, and the water was always cold. In a couple of minutes, he felt much better. His vision was no longer blurred, though he ached in every muscle and there still was no sound.

But his head was clear now and he could think straight.

He had to do something and do it quickly. He couldn't stay here. If someone found him, his ruse would be exposed. Barefooted, he couldn't travel far. He knew about where he was. Less than a mile back up the road toward town would be Adam Larabee's homestead. If he could get there, he'd be safe. Billy would help him explain to the family, and his secret would be kept.

He went back to the road and started walking. It was much easier walking than on the prairie, and there was less danger of stepping on a cactus. He saw a light flickering ahead and knew it must be either Larabee's or Meade's. A horse came down the trail. Matt, low to the ground, saw its outline against the sky and hurried off the trail, lying down in the grass close to the creek. As the horse galloped by he felt the tremble of the earth.

He hurried down the trail again, his spirits soaring, for now he knew the shock of the blast had deafened him only temporarily. The hollow, deathly stillness was no longer pressing in from every side.

At the lane which led to the light, he turned in. Once in the yard, he recognized Larabee's house, went to the door and knocked. Billy answered the knock.

"Matt!" he exclaimed. "Am I glad to see you! Papa just went down the road to see about that blast."

Matt grinned. The words Billy had said weren't clear, but he had managed to understand enough.

"He'll find a mess down there. I came mighty close to being there, too."

Mary Larabee came out and, in her efficient way, soon had Matt's scratches and bruises doctored. Digging the sliver out of his shoulder was too big an undertaking for her and, after attempting it, she shook her head.

"That's a job for the doc, Matt," she said. "Billy can bring him out tomorrow."

Matt shook his head. "Put a poultice on it. Maybe you can draw it out. I'd rather no one knew I was alive except you folks."

Adam came in half an hour later with a tale of the fantastic destruction of the wagon and everything around it. He was amazed to see Matt.

"I don't see how anything within fifty yards of that blast could walk away from it," he said.

"I just about didn't," Matt admitted. "I didn't intend to be that close. My horse fell."

"And never got up," Adam said. "That horse never knew what happened."

Billy was sent to town the next morning to find out what the reaction to the explosion was. He was to claim ignorance of everything pertaining to Matt and just watch and listen.

While he was gone, Tillie hobbled around, waiting on Matt hand and foot. Matt tried to do some things himself, but he saw instantly that he was offending the little girl.

"I can do as much as any girl my size," she declared.

"I don't want to be treated like a cripple."

"You're no cripple," Matt said. "You may have one leg a little shorter than the other, but up here," and he tapped his head, "where it really counts, you're in better shape than most people."

As the day wore on, Matt watched the lame girl. He was amazed at the things she had learned to do and the obstacles she had overcome. The one thing she couldn't do as well as most children was to move fast. The short leg and the defect in her back slowed her pace.

"Some day I'm going to get over this and be like other little girls," she told Matt. "Then I can run and play just like the others. And I can do more work and let Mama rest some. She works awful hard."

Matt nodded. "I know." He patted her head. "You're a big help to your Mama right now."

"I can do more, though, when I get so I can walk fast and run."

Matt tried out his muscles and found they were losing some of their soreness, due mostly, he thought, to the massaging Mary Larabee had given them last night and the lighter workouts Tillie had given him this morning. He marveled at the sunny disposition of the little girl. He had never seen any youngster, even one who was in perfect health, with such an optimistic outlook on life. Tillie, he saw, was the bright spot in Mary Larabee's humdrum life. Without the cheery smile and willing help of the crippled girl, Mary would have sunk to the depths of despair.

Billy came back to the homestead about mid-afternoon. And he was bursting with news. Matt met him at the door.

"Know what's happened to the mill?" Billy began.

"Burned?" Matt guessed.

Billy shook his head. "Preston Jok took it over. Said he held a mortgage on it and, since you were dead, he was taking over."

Matt nodded. "That's right. He's got the mortgage. But I didn't suppose he'd be in such a hurry to claim it."

"That ain't all," Billy added dramatically. "He's closing the mill. We can't get any more wheat ground."

Matt frowned. "How long does he figure to keep it closed?"

"He ain't ever going to open it, Sid Bolling says."

"Looks like we'll have to clear you of that murder charge fast," Adam Larabee said, "so you can get the mill running again."

Matt nodded. "I'll start on that tonight." But he was thinking more of the box in the back of the mill than he was of the wheat to be ground.

"You're in no shape to start gallivanting around," Mary Larabee put in.

"I'll have to start whether I'm ready or not," Matt said. "Anyway, you've got me back in top shape. I'll get along. Have you got a gun, Adam? I left town in a sort of hurry last night and didn't get any."

"All I've got is my rifle," Adam said. "I wouldn't

127

know how to use anything else."

Matt shook his head. "A rifle wouldn't be much help to me. I'll just stop in at the marshal's office when I get to town and borrow my own."

"You're going to town?" Billy gasped.

"That's the only place I can think of to start looking for the evidence to clear me. Dobson was killed there, and whoever is so set on seeing me hang is somewhere in Tumbleweed, I'll bet. If I'm going to find Dobson's real killer, I'm going to have to start looking there."

Adam nodded. "I reckon you're right. I found the other horse from your team of last night. He's out in the barn. You can take him or Billy's horse."

"Thanks," Matt said. "But I may pick up my own horse when I get to town, providing Jok hasn't moved him from the shed. Is John still at the mill?"

Billy shook his head. "Didn't see a sign of him. And nobody else had. When I started inquiring, I found out most people didn't even know he had been at the mill."

"Guess that's right," Matt mused. "John kept pretty much to himself."

Matt spent the rest of the afternoon lying on the cot in the living room at Larabee's. Yesterday's experience had made him bone weary. But supper time found him up and eager to be moving, excitement driving the tiredness out of his muscles.

He still wore his torn clothing, and instead of boots, he had a pair of Adam's old work shoes. He felt undressed with them, but they were more comfortable for walking. And he had decided to walk into town. It was only a trifle over a mile, and a horse would just be something to give him away when he got to Tumbleweed. Tonight's visit had to be a secret one. The only person he wanted to see was Dr. Henley. That sliver in his shoulder was hurting like blazes, though he didn't let the Larabees know it.

He was thankful he had decided to walk when, halfway to town, he heard a horse coming. Ducking off the trail, he hid in the tall river grass while Meade, a settler from down the creek, rode by on his way home. If Matt had ridden a horse, there would have been no hiding from him.

The town was quiet and for the most part dark when Matt came into the edge of town. He recalled the first night he had ridden in on this trail. These first houses had been dark that night, too. But he had been challenged then by a black-haired girl and warned of trouble ahead. He still remembered the beauty of that girl.

He jerked his thoughts back from their wanderings. There was a light in Henley's office down the street, and he wanted to get there before that light went out. He crossed the street, coming into the alley behind the buildings. The front of Henley's office was still lit up when he reached the back door. The door wasn't locked, and he pushed it open.

Henley wheeled at the sound, looking through the partition door. He paled as if he were looking at a ghost; then he left his chair and came into the back room.

"Matt!" he exclaimed. "I thought you were dead."

Matt held up a hand for silence. "I want people to think that. It came too near being the truth to be funny. I've got a sliver deep in my shoulder. Think you can get it out?"

"That's my business." Henley hung his coat over the one window in the back room, then closed the partition door and lit a lamp. "Tell me what happened?"

Matt quickly went over the details of what had happened since he had left the livery barn the night before. Henley built a fire, heating some water, and scalded a small needle-sharp knife.

"This will hurt a little, Matt, but it's the only way to get that sliver."

It did hurt, and Matt was relieved when the sliver came out. He flexed his arm, then turned to the back door.

"I'm going to pick up my guns at the marshal's office, then see what I can find out about Dobson's murder."

Henley nodded. "I'll keep my ears open. I'll be in my office for an hour or more yet writing letters. If you need anything, let me know."

"I'll do that," Matt promised, and waited till Henley blew out the lamp before opening the door.

There was only one way into the marshal's office, since the jail in the back of the building eliminated the possibility of a back door or back windows. He glanced up and down the street before stepping out on the boardwalk. The street was deserted, and Matt felt as conspicuous as a bull in a chicken pen.

He glanced at the window as he passed, then touched the door. To his surprise, the door opened. Guckert apparently was careless along with his many other faults. Or perhaps he thought, with no one in jail, there was no reason to lock the office.

Matt stepped inside and quickly closed the door. There was enough light from the street to help him find the desk. But finding his guns was another thing. He didn't light a match, for the marshal's office was right across the street from the hotel and a light here would almost certainly bring an investigation.

Eventually he found his gun belts hanging from a nail behind the desk. But the guns were missing. He lost another five minutes looking for the guns, which he finally found in a box in the opposite corner from the desk. Both guns were there, although he really hadn't expected to find but one. Evidently they were so certain that Matt was dead that they hadn't bothered to keep as evidence the gun they claimed had killed Dobson. That suited Matt.

He was just shoving the guns into their holsters when the door suddenly pushed inward. Matt froze, one gun still in his hand.

"Who's in here?" Matt recognized Guckert's heavy voice.

In the dim light Matt could see that Guckert had a gun in his hand. He was facing the desk, thinking, of

131

course, that any intruder would be there. Matt was at right angles to him and his eyes were already accustomed to the dark. Guckert's apparently weren't, for he was still moving toward the desk as if he were sure someone was there.

"Don't turn around, Guckert," Matt said softly, and Guckert stopped, uncertainty reflected in his quivering hands. "If you turn, it will be your last move. Drop your gun."

Reluctantly Guckert complied. "Who are you?" he croaked.

"Turn around now and see."

Slowly Guckert turned, his eyes trying to focus on Matt. His jaw dropped in horror as he recognized Matt. "A ghost!" he croaked.

"Afraid of ghosts?" Matt asked, grinning a little. Then he added quickly, "Don't try to run. This gun is no ghost."

"Wh—what do you want?"

Matt thought for a minute. Just what did he want to do with Guckert now that he had him? This wasn't in his plans. But there must be some way to use the big marshal. Then it struck him. Guckert was one of the men after the box down in the mill. He had been in on that hanging party last night, for he didn't put up any struggle to keep the mob out of the jail. And he was a coward. Matt had thought so before. Now he knew. Here might be a valuable source of information.

"Just tell me a few things, Guckert. Who killed Dandy Dobson?"

The marshal was silent for a minute; then he grunted almost incoherently, "You did."

Matt cocked the gun in his hand. "That's a lie, Guckert. Come on. Tell me who."

"I don't know," Guckert said.

Matt was stopped. Maybe Guckert didn't know. Maybe he was just stalling. Apparently he was sure Matt wouldn't shoot him if he didn't talk.

"Who worked up that mob last night?" Matt demanded.

But this time Guckert didn't say a word. He was sure of himself now. Matt hesitated a moment. He flinched as another pang shot through his shoulder. And that pain brought an idea to his mind.

"Come on, Guckert," he said. "Walk through that door slow. Turn down the side street north of here; then go up to Doc's back door."

"What for?" Guckert demanded, fear coming back into his voice.

"Because I say so," Matt said. "Don't think I won't shoot. I'm already wanted for murder. One more killing won't make it any worse."

That logic got through to the marshal and he shuffled out the door, with Matt just a step behind. A minute later Matt pushed open the rear door of Henley's office and shoved Guckert inside. Henley came through the partition door in surprise.

"You told me to come back if I needed any help," Matt said.

"What's he doing here?" Henley demanded,

pointing to the marshal.

"He's decided to tell me some of the things I want to know," Matt said.

"I ain't telling nothing," Guckert said sourly.

"I think he's got some meanness he needs to have cut out, Doc," Matt said. "Got that knife handy?"

Henley nodded, a light dawning in his eyes. "It's right here," he said, crossing to the table. "Sharp enough to give a close shave without any lather."

Matt watched the marshal. Guckert's eyes widened in fear as he watched Henley bring over the little knife. Guckert hadn't been too much afraid of a gun he was sure Matt wouldn't use, but a knife that could cut and not kill was something different.

"Doc used this on me to take out a sliver," Matt said, taking the knife from Henley. "I might not be as handy with it as Doc here, but I figure I can carve some pretty figures. I'm going to ask you some questions, Guckert. For every one you don't answer, I'm going to carve an initial on you. Understand?"

Guckert nodded, his eyes bulging as they followed every flourish of the knife. Matt turned the knife over slowly in his hand, the light from the lamp Henley had lit throwing shafts of light from the blade.

"Why did Jok take over my mill so soon?"

" 'Cause he thought you was dead," Guckert said.

"Why did he close it?"

Guckert swallowed. " 'Cause he wants to starve out the settlers and buy up their homesteads."

Henley caught his breath, and Matt was silent for a

moment. Bolling had been right. Jok had had a purpose in loaning him the money to buy the rollers for his mill. The mortgage gave him the mill and a stranglehold on the settlers.

"Why did he help the settlers if he wants to get rid of them?" Matt demanded.

Guckert, now that the secret was out, slumped forward in his chair, apparently ready to talk freely. "He wanted them to get the best land and live there at least a year. Then he planned to buy them out. Jok aims to own this whole valley, then sell it at his own price."

Matt nodded to himself. Things were fitting in nicely now. Last spring many of the settlers hadn't yet been on their land a year. Now their year was up and they could pay up their claims and get a clear title to the land. Jok would pay them enough to clear their land and have something to move out on. A clever scheme, and it was well on its way to success.

"Who worked up that mob last night? Jok?"

Guckert nodded without saying a word. Matt knew now who his real enemy was. He had thought it was the Sanfords, Bull and Gyp. And they had been his enemies while he ran the mill that kept the settlers prosperous. But Jok was the man he had to watch.

Suddenly it struck him that Dobson very likely had had the same idea that Jok had. From the prices he offered for the farmers' grain at his elevator, it looked as though he hoped to starve them out. And Dobson had had the money to buy out the settlers when they were ready to give up.

"Where did Jok expect to get the money to buy up the land?" Matt demanded.

Guckert grunted. "I don't know."

Maybe the marshal was telling the truth; maybe not. And then it struck Matt that Jok might have had a good reason for killing Dobson if they each had the same scheme.

"Did Jok kill Dobson?" Matt demanded.

Guckert sucked in his breath, then sank down in his chair with a scowl. "I don't know," he said.

"Then you must have killed him," Matt suggested.

"That's a lie," Guckert snapped. "I didn't kill him."

Matt considered using the knife as a threat to make Guckert tell who had killed Dobson, but in his own mind he knew now. And anyway, he needed more proof than just a confession forced from Guckert.

"Doc, have you got anything here that will let the marshal rest real well?"

Guckert's eyes widened in fear as he switched them from Matt to Henley.

"How long do you want him to rest?" Henley asked.

"Till sometime tomorrow, anyway. Maybe longer. He'd just be in the way running around."

"I see," Henley said. "I've got just what you want." He went into the front room of the office and came back in a minute with some white powder. "We'll give him some of this. I'll repeat the dose as necessary."

"Poison?" Guckert croaked.

Henley laughed. "Just something to make you sleep. You've been too active lately. You need rest."

Guckert balked at taking the powder, which Henley had put on some bread. But a flourish of the knife changed his mind. Before long, the marshal had dozed off to sleep.

"How long will that last?" Matt wanted to know.

"I'll stay over here tonight," Henley said. "When this wears off I'll give him some more."

"He can cause you a lot of trouble when he wakes up," Matt warned.

Henley grinned. "Not for a while after he's had that morphine. He'll rouse up as logger-headed as a bear coming out of hibernation. I'll ram some more down him before he comes to enough to balk."

"He looks pretty tame now," Matt said, looking at the sleeping marshal.

Henley nodded. "Just today I heard him bragging how he was going to clean up this place like Bat Masterson cleaned up Dodge City. He fancies himself as quite a gunman."

Matt went outside. His job now was to get positive evidence on Jok that would stand up in court. Guckert's confession, even if it were written down, would be thrown out of court because it had been obtained under stress. But it had cleared the air considerably for Matt. At least, now he knew who he was fighting and why.

But Jok still had the upper hand. For Matt was wanted for murder. Matt had no proof of his innocence, and the minute he showed himself, Jok would see to it he was arrested.

Matt had started toward the mill to get his horse when a whisper from the shadows stopped him.

"Matt, come here."

Matt recognized Bolling's voice even though it was barely audible. He stepped over into the shadows.

"What are you doing here?"

"I've been watching for things to break, thinking maybe I'd find out who did kill Dobson. I saw Guckert go into his office and I saw him come out with a gun in his back. I investigated."

"I'm glad to see you alive. I figured you didn't get out of the way of that dynamite."

"It was close. Find out anything about Dobson's murder?"

"No," Bolling said slowly. "But I did hear a shot that night right over north of me. If Dobson had been killed here in town instead of down by the lake, I'd say that might have been the shot that did it."

"I don't think he was killed by the lake," Matt said. "That's where his body was found. But just what would Dobson have been doing down by the lake in the middle of the night?"

"You're right," Bolling said positively. "I'll bet he was killed up here in town."

"In the hotel?" Matt asked.

Bolling shook his head. "I doubt it. Too many people there. The only building between my barn and the hotel is Jok's office."

"That ties in," Matt said quickly. "I've got it figured that Jok is the man who killed Dobson. I think I'll take a look at that office. Might find something."

Bolling nodded. "Good idea. But you'd better be careful. Jok has a room in the hotel, and it's right next door to his office."

Matt went down to the end of the street before crossing it. Then he came back behind the livery barn to the back of Jok's office. It was locked, but he managed to pry open a window. It squeaked as it yielded, and Matt waited for a minute, breathless, but there was no sound from the hotel. Matt squeezed through the window.

There was no light from the street filtering back to the rear of the office, and Matt had to take a chance, lighting a match and cupping it behind his hand. A quick search of the office showed nothing except some papers on the floor close to the back door. He caught his breath, however, when he kicked those papers aside. The floor was stained, and there was no question in Matt's mind as to what the stain was. He was convinced that Dobson had been killed right here in this office, but how could he prove it?

Suddenly he blew out his match. He had caught a scraping sound at the front of the office, like a key being turned carefully in the lock. Jok must have seen the light here in his office and come to investigate. Matt moved quickly to the window as he heard the lock fall back on the front door. Apparently Jok thought he could slip quietly in the front door and surprise the intruder in the back room.

Matt crowded through the window and dropped to

the ground outside just as he heard a yell from the front. A shot followed him as he ducked toward the back of the livery barn.

Matt didn't pause but cut back toward the road leading east out of town. The whole town would be awake in a minute, and if he borrowed a horse from Bolling he would be easy to follow. On foot, he could dodge pursuit in the darkness.

He had his proof now; at least in his own mind. But how was he going to use it to clear himself?

CHAPTER XIV

In spite of the objections of the Larabees, Matt went back to town the next morning. He wanted to ask Guckert some more questions. Last night he had been so interested in getting evidence against the man who had killed Dobson that he forgot about the little box down at the mill.

Guckert knew who was trying to get that box. Jok was the man who wanted to stop the mill from operating, but the man who wanted that box had other reasons for getting rid of Matt. And it wasn't just Matt who would suffer. Jennie stood to lose a fortune. That box was Matt's responsibility now. He had to see to it that Jennie got her rightful inheritance.

He found it easier to slip into town unnoticed than he had expected. He walked again, not wanting to bother to hide a horse when he got to town. He came to the back door of Henley's office, apparently without being seen. Henley was there, and stepped back in surprise when he saw him.

"What are you doing here at this time of day?" he demanded.

"Came to talk to Guckert. Some things I forgot to ask him last night."

Henley shook his head. "I'm afraid you'll have to wait awhile. He roused up about an hour ago, and I fed him a little more morphine. He won't be in a talking mood for quite a time."

Matt sank into a chair. "Then I'll just wait. I don't think anybody saw me come." He looked at the haggard lines in Henley's face. "Looks like you didn't sleep much last night. Guckert keep you awake?"

Henley shook his head. "I had something on my mind. I haven't slept much for a week."

"Something you want to talk about?"

Henley was silent for a minute. "It's nothing that will interest you," he said finally. "But I need somebody to tell me what to do."

"I'm no counselor, if that's what you need."

Henley rubbed a hand over his forehead. "I don't know what I need. Of course you know about Jennie and me, how we intend to get married and go back east where I'll start a city practice, probably in Philadelphia."

"I'd heard rumors to that effect. What's wrong with that?"

"Nothing except—" He stopped and ran a hand over his brow again. "Well, I've fallen in love with Suzy Jensen."

141

Matt suddenly felt like dancing. If Henley married Suzy, Jennie would be free and Matt could take advantage of that. But he checked his soaring spirits.

"How does Suzy feel about it, Doc? She's broken a dozen hearts."

"She feels just as I do. That's what's going to make it so hard to tell her."

"Tell her what?" Matt asked apprehensively.

"That my promise to Jennie still stands. I was foolish enough once to tell Suzy I'd give up everything for her. I would, too, except for my promise to Jennie. Jennie has stuck by me, and I won't let her down."

"Would that be fair to Jennie?"

"She'll never know, I promise you that. She'll be everything a man could ask for."

Matt couldn't argue with that, but he felt as frustrated as a hobbled colt wearing a blinder bridle. "How about Suzy?" he asked.

"She'll find someone else. She's had a dozen beaux before. She'll have a dozen more."

"Couldn't Jennie do the same?"

"She's not that type, Matt," Henley said, dropping his head into his hands. "She's pledged her loyalty to me and she'll never change. If the engagement is to be broken, I'll have to do it, and I won't be that kind of dog."

Matt nodded and said nothing more. There wasn't anything more to say. He admired Henley's loyalty. But he wished he could make him change his mind.

For he knew Jennie was just as loyal as Henley. They could very well go on with a marriage that neither of them wanted. But Matt admitted to himself that his belief that Jennie didn't want to marry Curt Henley was just wishful thinking on his part.

Then he thought of Jennie's inheritance and gave himself a mental kick. Even if Henley were out of the picture, Matt would be barred. That fortune would put Jennie far beyond his reach.

A horse came down the street, running hard, and Henley hurried to the window.

"Stopping here," he said. "You'd better get in the back room."

Matt stepped back and closed the door. He heard running footsteps come into the front of the office. He glanced at Guckert, who was breathing evenly, and wondered if that breathing could be heard out in the front office. Then he caught the first words out front and immediately forgot Guckert.

"You've got to go somewhere, Curt." It was Jennie's voice, and she was frightened.

"Why?" Henley demanded. "What happened to you, Jennie?"

"It's Gyp," Jennie panted. "He's coming to kill you."

Matt didn't wait for any more. He jerked open the door and stepped out. Jennie gasped when she saw him; then tears came and she sobbed almost hysterically.

"What's wrong, Henley?" Matt asked.

"Looks to me like somebody has beaten her," Henley said, his jaw hard and a frown on his face. "Probably Gyp. She says he's on his way to kill me."

Matt touched Jennie's shoulders. "Tell us what it's all about, Jennie."

But the first thing Jennie said when she lifted her face from her hands was, "I thought you were dead."

"I fooled a lot of people into thinking that. But what about Gyp?"

"He's insanely jealous over Suzy, Curt," Jennie said, turning back to the doctor. "He thinks you're weaning her away from him."

"He never had any hold on Suzy," Henley said fiercely.

"He thinks he did," Jennie said. "He killed Matt's brother in a fight over her. And now he's after you. You've got to run, Curt."

"I won't run," Henley said flatly. "Did he make those marks on your face?"

Jennie nodded. "I tried to stop him. I couldn't. So I got my horse and beat him here."

Matt looked at the two welts on Jennie's neck and cheek and the dark bruise at the edge of her hair. He felt his own blood running hot.

"I think I've got something to say about this," he said in a tight voice. "It was my brother that Gyp killed."

"This is my fight," Henley said. "He's coming after me."

"You're no gunhand," Matt said, and waved down

144

his protest. "I've had this chance coming to me for a long time."

"But you don't dare show yourself," Henley said.

Matt didn't retreat from his stand.

"They'll find out sooner or later that I'm still alive," he said.

Henley looked both relieved and determined. "A man doesn't let somebody else horn in on his fights just because he might not be big enough to take care of himself."

"You're not turning anything over to me," Matt said. "I've got first claim. If there's anything left of him when I get through, you can have him then."

Jennie suddenly faced Matt. "Doesn't anybody care what I think?" she said, her fists clenched.

Matt looked at her in surprise. "Are you afraid for us or Gyp?"

"I don't care what happens to Gyp. I'm afraid for you—both of you. You've got time to get away from here. If Gyp can't find Curt, he'll simmer around awhile, then cool off. Maybe there won't be any need for a fight then."

"I don't want him to cool off," Matt said. He felt he knew Gyp Sanford better than that. If Henley ran now, he could never show his face here again. Gyp wouldn't forget. The showdown was set for now. There was nothing to be gained by postponing it.

Jennie was watching him with an expression of horror in her eyes. "Are you a killer?"

Matt shot a glance at Henley, but the doctor had

nothing to say. Henley knew, Matt was sure, that this fight had to come and had to come now.

"A man can't run and expect to hold his head up afterwards," Matt said, his voice flat.

"That's what I've been telling you," Henley said. "It's my fight."

Henley was right. But Matt knew it would be suicide for the doctor to walk out to face Gyp. Gyp was a fast man with a gun. Fred had been no beginner, yet he hadn't been able to match Gyp.

"Look, Henley," Matt said, a note of finality in his voice. "Who's got the most reason for wanting to gun down Gyp—you or me? And who's got the better chance of coming back after he goes out to face him?"

Henley slumped in his chair and said nothing. Matt turned to Jennie, who was standing by the door, still breathing hard. "How far was Gyp behind you?"

"He's close," she said.

Matt checked his guns. After he got back to Larabee's last night, he had cleaned and oiled the one that had been thrown into the lake. It looked good, and he dropped it back in his left holster. His right gun he checked more thoroughly. That one would have to see him through this fight, for he wasn't a two-gun fighter. His left gun was just a spare.

Time grew heavy, lying like a tremendous weight on Matt's shoulders. The deep silence in the room added to the weight. Matt was startled when Jennie suddenly moved, leaving the door and coming over beside him.

"I'm scared," she confided.

146

He grinned a little. "Who isn't? I never faced a man like this before."

Henley leaned forward. "I thought you were a gunman."

Matt shook his head. "I quit before I got to that point. A couple of years ago I worked on a ranch in eastern New Mexico and we got into a scrap with a neighboring ranch. I was in half a dozen fights there. But it wasn't like this. Most of the time we didn't know just who we were shooting at. I began to work up a name, so I quit before I went too far."

Matt cocked an ear toward the street. There was no sound out there, not even the usual murmur of a lazy town going about its normal morning business.

"Must be coming," Matt said.

Neither Henley nor Jennie said anything.

Matt waited. It was still Gyp's move. Knowing the impatience that usually drove Gyp, he was sure that move wouldn't be long in coming. But it came with a sudden harshness that violated the deathly stillness that gripped the town.

"Henley!"

Just the one word, but it vibrated over the town and brought the doctor, pale-faced, out of his chair. Matt rose more leisurely and waved Henley back.

"Reckon he means me," he said softly.

Jennie touched his arm. "Good luck."

He nodded and grinned at her. He was glad she hadn't tried again to stop him. The time for that was past and she realized it. She was the kind who would steel herself to face the inevitable and never murmur.

Matt jerked his thoughts away from Jennie as he reached the door. There would be plenty of time later to think about her. And if there wasn't any more time for him, it wouldn't matter, anyway.

Gyp was standing spraddle-legged in the middle of the street down a way from the doctor's office. His eyes popped when he saw Matt.

"I thought you were dead," he grunted after a minute.

"You're wrong as usual," Matt said, stopping on the walk.

"I came after Henley."

"You'll have to wait your turn. First you're going to talk to me."

Gyp frowned. "What about?"

"You gave Jennie a beating this morning."

"She got in my way."

"I'm in your way now. Why don't you try beating me?"

Gyp crouched a little, a sneer twisting his face. "I've been waiting for this chance. I took care of Fred, all right."

Matt moved out into the street. He had to move a little to ease the tension that was gripping his muscles in an iron vise. He knew Gyp was fast with a gun; the fastest man in the valley, they said. And Gyp had faced men through gunsmoke before.

Matt was cold inside, his stomach muscles in a knot. Then he thought of Fred going down before the guns of this man, and he thought of Jennie being beaten this morning by him. And the muscles smoothed out a little and his fingers inched toward his gun.

Gyp was crouching like a big cat, turning slowly so as to keep facing Matt as he came into the street. Then suddenly, with a scream, he clawed for his gun. Matt saw the move coming and made his own draw. Matt's draw was fast, faster than anything Tumbleweed had ever seen. His gun roared first, and the bullet went true.

Matt felt dirt spurt up against his leg as Gyp's bullet plowed into the street. Then Matt was running forward. His gun roared again. He was barely aware of yelling:

"That's for Fred! And that's for Jennie!"

Then it was over. Matt stopped, looking down at the figure sprawled grotesquely in the dust. A sickness suddenly swept over him, and he turned and stumbled blindly toward the doctor's office.

Jennie met him at the door. "Are you hurt, Matt?"

Matt shook his head and stumbled into the office. "Just sick," he said, jerking off his gun belts and throwing them on the desk. "I don't want ever to see a gun again."

Henley took his arm. "You lie down here in the back room. You'll feel better in a few minutes."

"Is he hurt?" Jennie asked.

Henley shook his head. "Just exhausted. That nervous tension was harder on him than two days' work with no sleep. Well, I've got a job out in the street."

He clamped his teeth together and marched resolutely outside.

Matt didn't know how long he lay on the cot before he was jarred out of his despondent mood by an excited voice in the front office. His feet hit the floor when he recognized Billy's voice.

"Tillie's been hurt," Billy panted. "Come quick, Doc."

"What happened?" Jennie asked as Matt came through the partition door.

"She was carrying a bucket of water and fell somehow. I think she hurt her back."

"I'll be ready in a minute, Billy," Henley said.

"I'll go with you." Jennie reached for her hat.

Matt watched them get ready to go, thinking he should go with them. Then he remembered the box down in the mill. Everyone in Tumbleweed knew now that he was alive. Whoever wanted that box would speed up his efforts to get it—if he hadn't already found it.

"I've got something to give you, Jennie," he said as Jennie and the doctor started to leave the office. "I'll bring it to you down at Larabee's."

She nodded and went on, her mind apparently on the little crippled girl and not on what Matt had told her. Matt went out in the street and headed down toward the church and the road leading to the mill. If he could get that box to Larabee's, they would then somehow get it to Prairie Bend or McCook to a good lawyer who would probate the will and give Jennie her inheritance.

He stopped at the shed beside the mill. His horse was still there, and he saddled him. When he got that box, he wanted to turn it over to Jennie without the slightest delay.

The mill was deserted and the door unlocked. Matt didn't wonder about this. He doubted if John had locked it when he had left, and Jok probably had no key. The machinery was quiet, the way Jok intended to keep it.

But Matt paid no attention to the machinery now. He hurried past it to the back of the mill, dropping on his knees in front of the loose board. In a minute he was lifting the little steel box out onto the floor. He was just pushing the loose board back into place when a command froze his movement.

"Don't move, Freeman, and you won't get hurt."

Matt's fingers inched along his side toward his hip. Then he remembered he had thrown his guns on the doc's desk and hadn't picked them up again. Slowly he turned his head and met the blazing, eager eyes of Preston Jok.

Jok had a gun in his hand, and Matt didn't question his readiness to use it. If Jok was the man who had been trying to get his hands on this box, he certainly wouldn't stop at another murder now that he had the box practically in his grasp.

Jok moved forward slowly. "Stand up," he ordered. "Turn around."

Satisfied that Matt wasn't carrying a gun, Jok came closer. "Nice of you to find this box for me. I've

151

looked a long time for it."

"There's nothing in it that will do you any good," Matt said, trying desperately to think of some way to break out of this trap.

"Maybe. I think there is," Jok said. "Anyway, it will make no difference to you. You're supposed to be dead. Everybody thought you were."

"They know better now," Matt said.

"They can change their minds again. Put your hands behind you."

Reluctantly Matt obeyed. He had no choice, and until he could get a break, if he got one, he had to do as Jok told him. He heard Jok scraping around in the corner and presently felt a rope being wrapped around his wrists.

"Any reason for the bracelets?" Matt asked.

"I've got reasons for everything I do," Jok said boastfully. "Now lie down."

Matt dropped to his knees and rolled onto his back. "Going to tie my feet, too?"

Jok was at the back wall, opening the window there. When he turned back to Matt, he was grinning in wicked anticipation.

"I'll have to right now. But I doubt if it's really necessary. I don't think you could swim out of that waterwheel even with your feet free."

Matt knew then what was in Jok's evil mind. But Jok still had the gun and was only asking for an excuse to use it. Matt submitted to the rope around his ankles, then lay there while Jok went outside.

Desperately he tried to loosen some of the ropes in the short time Jok was gone, but the ropes hadn't slackened when he saw the waterwheel begin to turn. In another minute, Jok was back.

"I opened the gate wide," he said in satisfaction. "The wheel is turning at a good clip. You ought to have a nice ride on it."

Matt looked through the window. Obviously Jok intended to toss him through that. He'd probably land on the wheel as it was going up. By the time he went over the wheel and down through the water, he'd be pretty well chopped up. And if he did survive that, he wouldn't be able to get out of the swirling water just below the wheel. It would take a good swimmer to get out of that, and Matt would have his hands and feet tied.

"Nobody can say it was anything but an accident," Jok said.

"People don't tie themselves up like this and fall in the creek by accident," Matt said.

Jok nodded smugly. "So they don't." He glanced at his gun. "But a good clip on the head with this, and I can take the ropes off before you accidentally fall through that window."

Matt had no answer to that. He was cold inside, but it was a different coldness from that which had gripped him when he'd stepped out to meet Gyp this morning. He had had a chance to do something to help himself when he'd gone out against Gyp. Now he was helpless.

He watched Jok slowly turn the gun around in his hand, bringing the butt forward like a club.

CHAPTER XV

Matt drew himself up, ready to put up a struggle when Jok got close enough. But Jok didn't come that close. A sharp command from behind brought him to a halt.

"Don't move, Jok, or I'll blast you."

Matt wheeled his eyes back to the man who stood half hidden in the noisy machinery. "John!" he exclaimed.

Jok wheeled then, his eyes boring into the little man. "John Kent! I thought you had sense enough to get out of this country."

"You tried to kill me that night in your office. But you only blinded me in one eye. The other eye is good enough to see to kill you."

"You haven't got the nerve to kill me," Jok said, quickly recovering from his surprise.

"Don't try to stop me or I'll show you," John said.

Matt watched him, fascinated. The little man was scared to the marrow of his bones. It showed in his good eye and in the trembling of his hand. But a frightened man is sometimes a dangerous man, and apparently Jok decided to wait for a chance to over-power him.

John, however, had other ideas. "Back up, Jok. So help me, I'll kill you if you don't." Then, as Jok obeyed, he added. "Now don't move. I'm going to get that box."

"It won't do you any good," Jok said.

"It will do my soul some good to see you beat out," John said. "I may have been the black sheep of the Kent family and no good, but I'm not going to see my sister's girl cheated out of everything. Keep back."

John moved forward slowly, stooping to pick up the box. His eyes never left Jok, and his gun remained as steady as his trembling hand could hold it. When he had the box under his left arm, he began retreating.

Matt had hoped that John would untie him. But John was probably too frightened to notice that Matt was even present. His fear of Jok must be a horrible thing, Matt decided. He thought of asking John to take the ropes off him but, looking at Jok, he knew that the slightest break in John's watchfulness would bring the lawyer into action. And Matt doubted John could handle Jok right now if Jok undertook to take the box from him.

John backed out of sight behind the machinery, and Matt heard his running feet as he left the mill. He turned his eyes on Jok to see what the lawyer would do now. He was still at Jok's mercy. But the lawyer seemed to have forgotten him. Apparently that box meant everything to him. He went after John, running hard.

Matt turned his attention to the ropes holding him. He was sure that John wouldn't get far with that box before Jok overtook him. And then Jok would have the box again.

Matt jerked himself up to his knees, then lurched to his feet. There might be something here he could use to cut his ropes, but he didn't know where. Up front in his living quarters, he could get a knife.

It was slow work hopping past the stands of rollers, being careful not to fall into a flying belt. But he finally made it to the little room where he had lived since coming to Tumbleweed. Nothing seemed to have been moved.

It was only a matter of a minute till Matt had backed up to his little table and pulled open a drawer. He fished out a butcher knife and worked it around in his fingers until the blade was pressed against the ropes.

He slashed his skin several times before the ropes finally fell away. It took only seconds then, to get the ropes off his feet. Running outside, he looked to left and right before a groan brought his eyes to focus on the hitchrack. Lying there, blood on the side of his head, was John Kent. Matt ran to him.

"What happened?"

John sat up, holding his head with both hands. "I couldn't get away. I knew I couldn't."

"What did he hit you with?" Matt asked, looking at the head wound with concern.

"His gun," John said, his strength rapidly coming back. "Afraid to shoot me, I guess. Too much noise. You've got to catch him, Matt, and get that box away from him."

"What good will it do him?" Matt took out his big handkerchief and started wrapping it around John's head.

"He wants to destroy it. It's a later will than the one he persuaded Molly to make out, leaving him the Lazy K and all her money. I found out about that one and showed Molly how wrong she was. She made this will just a while before she died. Then before we could get a lawyer to probate it, there was a robbery at the Lazy K and the box with the will was stolen."

Matt continued to work with the bandage. "Jok did it?"

"I think so. He thought he'd killed me then. Somebody in Jok's crew stole the box from him and left it with your brother, then ran off with the key. He was killed."

"I got the key," Matt said, trying to knot the handkerchief. "I suppose if Jok can destroy this will leaving everything to Jennie, the other will leaving the property to him will be good?"

John nodded. "Exactly. He's having it probated now. It will be final in another month unless we produce this later one."

"But why did she make out the will to Jok?"

"He was her husband. Jok is Jennie's father, and he persuaded Molly, when Molly was sick and knew she wouldn't live long, that if she'd leave everything to him, he'd take care of Jennie. Molly was born gullible or she wouldn't have married Jok in the first place."

Matt barely heard the last part of John's explanation.

His mind stuck on the revelation that Jok was Jennie's father. "Does Jennie know who her father is?" he asked.

"No. Molly ran off from Jok when Jennie was only a baby. She never told her. You'd better go after Jok now."

Matt snapped out of his surprise. "Where do you think he went?"

"I'd guess to his office. He won't throw the box away, because there are some negotiable bonds in it. And he doesn't have the key, so he'll have to force open the box."

"Will you be all right?"

John nodded. "Sure. Anyway, I'd rather stay here and die than see Jok get away with his scheme."

Matt ran to the shed and got his horse, then headed him up the slope toward town. His mind was racing, trying to piece together parts of the picture that he hadn't seen before. There was fifty thousand dollars in money in Molly Kent's estate. Apparently that was where Jok expected to get the money to buy out these settlers along the creek. Once he controlled this valley and this town, he could set himself up as king and nobody could challenge him.

Matt pulled into the alley behind the doctor's office. He needed his guns again now. The last hour had driven the gunsmoke sickness from him. The door was unlocked, for Henley had left in a hurry to go to the aid of little Tillie Larabee.

Inside, Matt found Guckert tossing uneasily on the

floor in the back room. The effect of the morphine was evidently wearing off. Well, no matter. There was nothing to be gained by keeping Guckert drugged any longer. Matt picked up his guns and went out the front door. He ran across the street to the back of the hotel and came up to Jok's office from the rear.

Moving quietly to the window, he peered in and saw the lawyer bending over the box on his desk, working diligently to pry open the lid. With a stroke of the gun in his hand, Matt broke the glass of the window.

"Hold it, Jok," he snapped. "Hand over that box."

Jok had wheeled at the sound of breaking glass, and now he stood rooted to the floor, breathing hard, the look of a cornered animal in his eyes.

"Come and get it if you want it," he said finally.

Matt considered the situation. The door would be locked. A careful man like Jok would lock both front and back doors before he started on a job such as burning a will. Matt could have shot Jok, but it wasn't in him to do that when Jok wasn't fighting. And Jok realized that.

There was only one thing to do. Using the gun barrel, Matt knocked all the glass out of the window frame. He didn't dare take his eyes off Jok long enough to try the door or shoot open the lock. When the glass was out, he started through the window, trying to keep the gun on Jok. But he had to duck his head to get it through the window, and in that instant Jok struck.

Matt heard him coming. With a push from the leg

still outside the window, Matt catapulted himself inside, his head burying itself in the lawyer's stomach. The breath exploded from Jok, but he managed to plant a foot in Matt's ribs as he fell away. Pain ripped up Matt's side as he rolled over and got to his feet.

He found Jok already on his feet and charging down on him. The lawyer was almost the same size as Matt, but his muscles were not work-hardened. Nevertheless, he was fighting like a demon, and Matt, struggling against the pain in his side as well as against the lawyer, had to give ground.

Desperation was driving Jok. All the scheming of the last year and a half was threatened now by Matt. Matt could see in Jok's face the frantic determination to wipe out that threat.

Matt reeled back against the wall from a fist that caught him on the side of the head. He felt himself slipping down the wall and fought to keep on his feet. He didn't dare give Jok a chance to get to his gun.

Dimly he saw the lawyer dive to his desk. But he didn't come up with a gun. He snatched the box off the top of the desk and ran through the partition door. Matt struggled to his feet as he heard the key rasp in the lock out front. Gathering strength, he plunged through the partition doorway just as the outside door came open.

Diving forward, Matt caught Jok's feet and threw him hard in the doorway. The lawyer rolled over and lashed out with both his feet, catching Matt on the chin with one heel. Matt's hold was broken and he rolled groggily to his feet. But Jok was already up and running wildly into the street. Matt started after him, then noticed suddenly that he had left the box where it had fallen beside the open door.

Then he saw that Jok wasn't abandoning the box. Outside the doctor's office, still a little unsteady on his feet, was the marshal.

"Get that box, Pete," Jok yelled as he approached the marshal. "I'm going to blow up the dam."

Pete Guckert shook his head as if to clear it of a mist. "What for?"

"Do what I tell you," Jok yelled, and ran past him.

Matt started into the street. Jok must have some scheme to blow up the dam. That would send a wall of water sweeping down on the homesteads below. And Larabee's would be the first one hit. Surely Jok must know that Jennie was at Larabee's. Destroying Jennie would be the next best thing, in Jok's greedy, hate-crazed mind, to destroying the will.

A horse pounded into town past Bolling's livery barn. Matt shot a glance that way and stopped as he saw Suzy Jensen bearing down on him. She jerked her horse to a halt beside him.

"Where's Curt?" she demanded.

"He went down to Larabee's. Tillie's hurt."

Suzy kicked her horse into a run again. "Gyp's after him," she called back. "I've got to tell him."

Then she was out of earshot before Matt could tell her what had happened. His attention came back to his immediate job. He had to stop Jok, who was running past the church now on his way down the slope to the dam.

But as he started down the street, Pete Guckert came out to intercept him. He was still groggy from the morphine, but his mind was rapidly clearing and his muscles regaining their coordination. When Matt found him blocking his path, he stopped.

"What's Jok going to do?" he demanded.

"Light the dynamite we put in the dam the first day he took over," Guckert said, wiping a hand over his head.

"That will cause a flood," Matt said, starting forward again.

Guckert grabbed his arm and threw him back. "That's what he aims to do. He said he'd drown out the settlers if he couldn't get them to leave any other way."

Matt charged forward again, only this time he didn't try to go around the marshal. He drove straight into him. He was tired and his side hurt, but Guckert was still a little groggy from his long enforced sleep. Every minute Matt delayed would work against him now. Jok was getting closer to the dam, and Guckert was rapidly shaking off the effects of the drug.

Guckert struck out with a fist, but Matt weaved around it and came on, slamming two hard blows to the marshal's jaw. Guckert reeled back and Matt followed with a rain of hard, smashing drives on the marshal's face. It was like trying to kill a bull with a willow switch, it seemed to Matt. Guckert had lost his ability to fight back after those two first blows jarred

162

his already scrambled senses. But still he stood in Matt's way and blocked him from going after Jok.

Then, as Guckert made a feeble pass at Matt, Matt caught him at the base of the ear with a blow that had all his remaining strength behind it. The marshal, going forward toward Matt, kept on going. And when Matt stepped aside, he sprawled in the dust, quivered once, and lay still.

Matt wheeled and ran toward the dam. But he was just at the church at the top of the slope when the explosion came. Earth and water spouted into the sky beside the mill. Matt watched for an instant in fascinated horror.

Tuttle came running out of the church yard where he had been working around some puny flowers growing in a little pot there.

"The dam!" he cried. "Everybody downstream will be drowned."

Matt saw the wall of water pouring through the huge hole ripped in the face of the dam. He broke the spell gripping him and wheeled toward his horse, still standing behind the doctor's office where he had left him. As he got his horse, he saw Tuttle hurrying toward a blaze-faced sorrel standing by his house behind the church.

Then Matt remembered the box. Driving his horse into the main street, he guided him over by Jok's office, spending precious seconds to stop and get the box. He also picked up the gun he had lost during his fight with Jok and jammed it back in its holster. Then he mounted again and spurred his horse to the east along the river bank.

He glanced at the wild water coming down the creek bed in a four-foot wall, devouring everything in its path like a hungry dog gulping meat scraps, and reaching slimy fingers out over the banks, searching for more food for its voracious appetite.

Matt watched the water's progress as he drove his horse on. The continued pressure of the water stored up in the dam kept the flood advancing at a fast pace. Too fast, Matt thought in desperation, for him to get to Larabee's in time to warn him of his danger.

CHAPTER XVI

At first Matt couldn't gain much on the rampaging water. Then, as it advanced farther from the pressure exerted by the water pouring out of the dam, it lost a little of its speed. He had a chance now, he thought, to get to Larabee's ahead of the flood. But still he doubted if he could get everyone to safety. There would be seven people there now, the way he figured it. The doctor and Jennie had had plenty of time to make it, and Suzy would be there, too, by now, judging by the way she had been riding when she left town.

Once, glancing back at the flood, Matt caught a glimpse of a horse and twisted to get a good look. It was Jok, and he had a fast horse, faster than Matt's. Apparently he figured Matt had taken the box and he was coming after it.

Matt spurred his horse harder. He had Jok to beat now as well as the flood. And Jok was gaining much faster than the water. Then, whipping a glance back at Jok, he saw another horse farther back. A blaze-faced sorrel. Mark Tuttle.

The creek took a sharp bend just above Larabee's farm. After driving straight at the building, it suddenly veered almost at right angles to the north for fifty yards, easing back to an easterly course beyond the farm buildings. At the turn, the ground on the south side of the creek rose to a bank several feet higher than the bank either above or below it.

Matt was just topping this rise, more than a hundred yards ahead of the water, when his horse stumbled and fell. Matt, caught completely by surprise, was thrown hard. The horse lunged to its feet and ran off to the south.

For an instant Matt was too stunned to try to get up. Then, when he did push himself to a sitting position, he saw Jok bearing down on him like a stampeding bull.

Before Matt could get to his feet, Jok came alongside and, without reining in his horse, left the saddle in a long dive. Matt would have been crushed into the ground if the lawyer's aim had been as deadly as his intentions. But he barely brushed Matt as he thudded into the ground, and Matt rolled away, scrambling to his feet.

Jok, apparently unhurt, was jumping to his feet, too. Matt drove into the lawyer before he got his balance.

He had to end this in a hurry. The water was slamming into the turn directly below them now and in another minute would spread out over the flat below, engulfing the Larabee buildings.

But Jok had the strength of a wild bull, and he wrapped his arms around Matt, throwing them both to the ground. This was Jok's last stand, his last chance to succeed with his scheme. The realization of it was in his eyes and in the desperation with which he fought.

The roar of the angry water just below was in Matt's ears as he fought to break Jok's grip on him. Jok brought up a knee and tried to gouge Matt with it. But Matt caught the leg and wrenched the foot up almost in Jok's face. Then he began to apply all the pressure he could master.

Jok gritted his teeth against the pain and jabbed a hand into Matt's face, his fingers seeking Matt's eyes. One finger slipped between Matt's parted teeth, and Matt clamped down. Jok screamed in pain, a sound that was lost a few feet away in the roar of the water.

The lawyer jerked his hand free, and the extra strength generated by the pain gave him the advantage. He broke Matt's hold on his leg. They rolled apart, but before Matt could get to his feet, Jok was on him again.

Matt was looking for trouble this time, however. As Jok dove at him, Matt brought his knees up quickly, catching Jok on the side of the head. The lawyer rolled off Matt's legs, and Matt scrambled to his feet. Only then was he aware that the other rider had caught up with them.

Matt glanced around as Jok lay on the ground, not unconscious, but unable to get up and resume the fight. Surprise washed over Matt as he saw not Mark Tuttle, but John Kent, climbing off the horse.

"I borrowed this horse from the preacher," John explained. "I had to see what I could do to save Jennie. Looks like you might need me here."

Matt glanced at Jok, on his hands and knees now. Then he looked down at the buildings below. Water had spread out over the flat, was lapping the sides of the buildings. But there was no sign of the seven people he knew must be down there.

Matt jerked his gun out of his holster. "Watch Jok," he said. "I'll take care of him later."

"If he's still here," John said in a tone that guaranteed Jok wouldn't escape.

Matt ran to Tuttle's horse, which was the closest animal. He heard John behind him giving orders to Jok.

"Take this pencil and paper and write down who killed Dobson. Then get over there on the edge of that bank and stand there where I can watch you."

Matt swung up on the horse, uncoiled the rope that Tuttle apparently had just tied there in preparation for a rescue mission. Matt spun around as he heard a gun boom. Jok, his face blanching, was slowly backing to the point of land directly above the roaring water.

"The water," Jok screamed. "It's washing out this bank."

"Stand right there," John said determinedly. "I'll kill you if you make a move."

Matt drove the sorrel down the slope into the water. The horse reared when he felt the swift water tugging at his legs, but he responded to Matt's urging. The water was already two feet deep outside the house when Matt got to the door. Beyond the house the barn was over half inundated. The horses were loose and scrambling out of the water toward the slope to the south. Some chickens had made it to the higher ground to the south, some were perched on top of the barn, and some were floating down the river on their way to destruction.

Matt reached the door, holding the rope which had one end fastened securely to the saddle horn. Adam Larabee was floundering through the door, the water almost knocking his legs from under him. He had been trying to help his wife, but his strength was just enough to hold himself up. The back door of the house had just been broken open by the flood and the water was racing through the house with the same speed with which it was spreading over the entire bottom land.

Billy had been thrown against the side of the house, and Henley was holding him, trying to steady him on his feet. Jennie and Suzy were holding Tillie between them and trying to struggle to the door.

"Put Billy on the horse, Doc," Matt yelled above the roar of the water, which was increasing every minute as more water poured onto the flat.

Henley struggled to the door, supporting Billy, who was working just as hard to free himself of the doctor's support as he was to overcome the tug of the water against his legs.

Matt turned to the girls, lifting Tillie in his arms. "Everybody get hold of that rope," he ordered.

Henley came back to Matt as the others took a grip on the rope. Billy was in the saddle looking back, waiting for orders. "Hold the rope behind me, Doc," Matt said. "Head for high ground, Billy."

Matt found that holding Tillie and keeping up with the others was a big job. Tillie was light, but as she had an injured back, she couldn't be handled carelessly. Henley helped him from behind, and both Jennie and Suzy gave him support when they could.

Matt glanced back once before they reached dry ground and saw the little soddy begin to crumble. The flood was eating it away, dissolving it like sugar in a pan of water.

Just as they reached the edge of the water and safety, Matt twisted his head at the sound of a shot, a sound almost drowned by the roar of the water. For a minute he had forgotten John out there on the knoll holding Jok at gunpoint. They were both standing about as he had last seen them, except that Jok was waving his arms desperately and John was holding the gun ready to shoot again.

Then Matt saw it happen. The ground under Jok crumbled, and with a scream that carried above the roaring voice of the flood, the lawyer disappeared into the churning water. Matt glanced along the rope to see how many others had witnessed Jok's disappearance. Apparently none had. Safety was so sweet to them that they were oblivious to everything else.

Matt laid Tillie down gently on the dry ground and turned back to the raging river. But there was no sign of Jok.

Matt went out to meet John. John's face was colorless and there was something akin to horror in his eyes, yet his jaw was set in a rigid line as if defying Matt to chastise him.

"Jok started that flood to kill somebody," John said tightly. "And the river was entitled to its reward."

Matt nodded, looking back at the river and the place where Larabee's homestead had been located. Only two big whirling eddies marked the spots where the house and barn had been. "I reckon you're right, John. Ride to town, will you, and bring out a wagon to take these people back?"

"Sure," John said. "Here's your gun, Matt, and a confession Jok signed."

Matt took the gun and the paper. The paper contained only five words. "I killed Dobson, Preston Jok." But those five words meant a lot to Matt. He put the paper in his pocket and stood looking down at the gun in his hand a minute before dropping it back in its holster. Fred's guns. Fred hadn't been able to finish the fight, but his guns had seen the bitter end.

Mark Tuttle turned the church into a community

hotel and makeshift hospital, inviting all the settlers who had lost their homes in the flood. As far as Matt could learn as he moved around the church, only the man who had started the flood, Preston Jok, had died in it.

The despair that had gripped the settlers as they came into town was slowly changing to hope as they heard the story and realized that the ones who had caused their troubles were gone. Plans for rebuilding their homes and the dam were made before the men dropped off to sleep that night. The mill was all right, and Matt told them the dam could be completed in time to grind their wheat this fall. And the settlers who had escaped the flood volunteered to help the unfortunate ones rebuild.

John had worked faithfully with Matt and Henley throughout the afternoon, getting everyone comfortable and the few minor injuries patched up. Jennie had recognized her uncle while he worked and scolded him for not letting her know he was here in town.

Matt had remembered to go to the high point of ground and pick up the box he had dropped there. He had put it in Henley's office, feeling sure now that it would be safe. Nevertheless, he was in a hurry to turn it over to Jennie. So when supper was over and the homeless farmers in the church were settling down for the night, Matt called Jennie over.

"I've got something down in Doc's office for you, Jennie."

Jennie, her eyes shining and looking prettier than

Matt thought she had a right to look, smiled mischievously. "Can't you give it to me here?"

Matt shook his head. "It's a box your mother left for you. It's been the cause of a great deal of the trouble here."

Jennie frowned a little. "I don't understand, Matt."

"The box will explain," he said, leading Jennie outside.

He glanced down at the girl walking close beside him toward Henley's office. For an instant an almost overwhelming desire to throw away the box still unlocked swept over him. Right now he might have this girl. She was what he wanted more than anything in the world. But in a few minutes this girl wouldn't exist. In her place would be a rich girl, a girl who would have wealth enough to go anywhere she wanted and buy anything she wanted. Certainly anything in Tumbleweed would be unworthy of her consideration.

But now, before she saw that box and its contents—His hand strayed over and touched her arm, and he jerked it back as if he'd been burned. He had no right even to dream of such things. This girl would soon be gone.

But Jennie hadn't missed his move. She glanced at him with a look that was both inviting and inquisitive.

"What will Bull do now that Gyp is gone?" Matt asked, trying to find a subject about which he felt sure of himself.

"Nothing," Jennie said. "Bull's not such a bad man. It was Gyp who was crowding him all the time. The only man left who might cause trouble, it seems to me, is Pete Guckert."

Matt shook his head. "He'll give no trouble. He was Jok's tool. He hasn't been seen since the flood. And I doubt if he'll ever be seen around here again."

Matt led the way inside Henley's office and lit the lamp. Then Jennie stopped him.

"Matt, there's something I want to tell you. Suzy and I are friends now. When the flood came today she showed what she's really made of. She admitted that she's really in love with Curt. And he's in love with her, too."

Matt cleared his throat. "I know. But what about you?"

"I don't want a man who doesn't love me. Besides, I—"

Her voice trailed off, and Matt fought to keep from telling her what was surging up in him, almost choking him. He turned to the box, fished out the key and unlocked it.

"Read what's in there, Jennie. It will change everything for you."

He went to the window and stared out into the night; the darkness was broken only by feeble lights from windows along the street. For what seemed an eternity, she read. Then he heard the lid close on the box.

"That does change things," she said softly. "I didn't know about this. The first thing I'm going to do when I get that money is to send Tillie away for an operation on her back."

"Maybe Henley will change his mind now," Matt suggested.

Jennie smiled. "He won't. He's not like that. Anyway, I won't give him a chance. But I am going to set him up in a good office, right here. Both he and Suzy want to stay here. Anyway, I want a good doctor for my family."

"You won't be staying here now," Matt said.

"Why not? I've got a big ranch to run." She crossed to the window where he was still standing. "Uncle John can soon learn to run the mill now that he's been there for a while. Billy can help him. I suppose Ken Yost, the Lazy K foreman, is taking care of the ranch now. We'll probably keep him. You know how to run a ranch, don't you?"

Matt wheeled on her. "Jennie, you don't know— You haven't had time to think about what you'll do with all that money."

Tears suddenly welled into her eyes. "Matt," she cried, "do I have to propose to you?"

He shook as if with a chill. This wasn't the way it ought to be. But he felt his resistance crumbling as the sod walls of Larabee's house had crumbled in the face of the water's assault today. His arms went around her and he kissed her with all the love of a starving heart.

Then he released her and stepped back, looking down into her eyes, sparkling with misty tears. "I wanted to ask you, Jennie," he said softly. "But I didn't think I had the right."

"I knew what you were thinking," she said, smiling.

"How did you know?"

"I've been teaching school, remember? I can usually tell from looking at a little boy's face what he's thinking."

"I'm no little boy," he reminded her sternly.

She laughed. "No. You're a big boy. But I still know what you want. Now kiss me again."

He really had no choice but to obey. And he'd have been the most disappointed man in the world if he'd had any other choice.

Center Point Publishing
600 Brooks Road • PO Box 1
Thorndike ME 04986-0001 USA

(207) 568-3717

US & Canada:
1 800 929-9108